"Have you heard about our engagement?"

Holly's cheeks went the same shade of pink as the peonies on display in the window. "I had nothing to do with that tweet. Kendra sent it before I could stop her." She bit her lip. "I'm sorry if it's embarrassed you. If we ignore it, hopefully it will go away."

"What if I told you I didn't want it to go away?"

Her big brown eyes rounded. "What?"

Zack leaned down to smell the vase of roses sitting on the counter. He straightened and gave her a winning smile. "What if it suited me to be engaged for a while?"

Melanie Milburne read her first Harlequin novel at the age of seventeen, in between studying for her final exams. After completing a master's degree in education, she decided to write a novel, and thus her career as a romance author was born. Melanie is an ambassador for the Australian Childhood Foundation and a keen dog lover and trainer. She enjoys long walks in the Tasmanian bush. In 2015 Melanie won the HOLT Medallion, a prestigious award honoring outstanding literary talent.

Books by Melanie Milburne

Harlequin Presents

The Tycoon's Marriage Deal
A Virgin for a Vow
Blackmailed into the Marriage Bed
Tycoon's Forbidden Cinderella

Conveniently Wed!

Bound by a One-Night Vow

One Night With Consequences

A Ring for the Greek's Baby

The Ravensdale Scandals

Ravensdale's Defiant Captive
Awakening the Ravensdale Heiress
Engaged to Her Ravensdale Enemy
The Most Scandalous Ravensdale

Melanie Milburne

CLAIMED FOR THE BILLIONAIRE'S CONVENIENCE

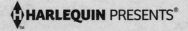

HARLEQUIN PRESENTS®

Recycling programs
for this product may
not exist in your area.

ISBN-13: 978-1-335-47799-6

Claimed for the Billionaire's Convenience

First North American publication 2018

Copyright © 2018 by Melanie Milburne

Printed in U.S.A.

CLAIMED FOR THE
BILLIONAIRE'S
CONVENIENCE

To Bernice (B) Dodds. You have been a part of my journey as a writer from my very first RWAustralia conference. I am so glad we are friends and writing colleagues. This one is for you with much love. Xxxxx

CHAPTER ONE

EVERY TIME HOLLY FROST looked at her younger sister's engagement party invitation she wanted to emigrate. To Siberia. Not because she didn't love her baby sister Belinda. She did. She loved all three of her sisters—Katie, Meg and Belinda were awesome. The best sisters a girl could ask for. Holly loved her parents too, and her grandparents. She'd been lucky in the family lottery, unlike a couple of her friends who had the sort of families you read about in crime novels. All of Holly's family were supportive and loving. Katie and Meg were happily married, and now Belinda was joining them, which left Holly the odd one out.

Again.

Her baby sister was getting married, which meant everyone would look at Holly and ask when she was going to find herself a husband. Argh. Like she needed another man in her life after being jilted not once, but twice.

How could she get through another family gathering with no partner in tow? How could she bear the looks and pointed questions about her lack of a love life? Her family thought any young woman pushing thirty should have a husband on the horizon if not in hand. Especially if said young woman was a wedding florist and was surrounded by blissfully happy brides every day of the week, and yes, even on weekends.

Double argh.

Holly was the go-to wedding florist in London. Obsessed by all things bridal since childhood, she had built her business on wedding flowers. She also did flowers for funerals, parties, corporate functions and so on, but it was her wedding work that had lifted her profile. She'd done the flowers for a minor celebrity's marriage four years ago. The reality-TV star had more followers on social media than the Kardashians.

Holly's shop was her life. She didn't have time for anything else. Being successful professionally made up for not being successful personally. Her failed relationships were as bad as having dead flowers on display in her shop window. Withered hope, dried-up dreams, bruised ego.

Why her family thought she couldn't possibly be happy remaining single was a constant source of frustration to her. Plenty of people were happy being single. Lots and lots of people were single and loving it. Not everyone wanted the fairy tale. The fairy tale sucked if your handsome prince decided to run off with another woman the week before your wedding. It sucked even more if your second handsome prince—because who didn't try things twice to see if they could get it right the second time?—also took off. But this time on the day before the wedding with his personal trainer.

Holly had been cured of fairy-tale fever by two fickle fiancés.

Permanently cured.

'Will you be doing the flowers for your sister's wedding?' Jane, her chief assistant asked, coming in from the cool room with a bunch of white roses.

Holly cleared a space on her workbench for the roses. 'Yep. And I'm chief bridesmaid. Again. Go me.'

'Three times a bridesmaid…' Jane stepped back as if she were trying to avoid contamination by association. 'Glad it's you and not me. Aren't you worried you might jinx your chances of—'

'No.' Holly picked up one of the roses and snipped the stem. 'Because I don't want to get married.'

'Don't you want to have one more go? To see if this time—'

'Nope.' Holly took another rose and snapped off the stem. 'I do not.'

Jane glanced at the invitation on Holly's desk. 'So who will be your plus-one for Belinda's engagement party?'

Holly wrapped fine green wire around the stem of a rose like she was tying up one of her cheating exes. 'I'm not taking anyone.'

Jane gave a series of exaggerated blinks. 'You're going alone? To one of your family's parties? Isn't that a bit…erm, risky after the last time?'

Holly pressed her lips together so hard she could have cracked concrete. 'I told my mother in no uncertain terms she is to refrain from setting me up with techie nerds. The ones with dandruff who get blind drunk because they're nervous about meeting a real woman in the flesh instead of an avatar on a computer screen. I'm fine being single.' She picked up another rose and began wiring it. 'Just because everyone in my family is partnered doesn't mean I want to be.'

'Speaking of the absence of partners…' Jane handed over the printout of a new order that had come in overnight via the website. 'You've been asked to do the flowers for a divorce party. That's a first, isn't it?'

Holly frowned and peered at the form. 'Hmm, that's from Kendra Hutchinson. She was one of my brides about four years ago, before you came to work for me. Big socialite wedding. Massive. I paid off my overdraft with that account. I was up two nights in a row doing the flowers. I knew she was wasting her time marrying that guy. She knew he was getting it on with one of the bridesmaids but she still went ahead with the wedding. She was so blinded by love she needed a guide dog. No. Two guide dogs and a white cane.'

'Weddings are expensive things to cancel at the last minute.'

'Tell me about it.' Holly grimaced and snipped off another stem. *And dead embarrassing.*

'Do you know who handled Kendra's divorce?' Jane's tone and twinkling eyes were straight out of the schoolyard gossip handbook. 'Zack Knight, the celebrity divorce lawyer who's made his millions by dissolving peoples' marriages. Maybe you'll meet him at the party.'

Holly stretched her lips into a smile that felt like it belonged on a corpse. 'I'll look forward to it.' *Not.*

Jane's expression lost some of its sparkle when she looked at the divorce party order printout again. 'I hope we're not going to only do divorce parties and funerals now…'

A clench of panic gripped Holly's gut like a bad case of giardia. During the last week, three of her biggest clients had cancelled their wedding bookings without explanation. It had never happened before and she was trying not to worry. Yet. But she had a mortgage and expensive renovations on her new house to pay for. Staff to pay. Hell to pay if she failed. 'It'll be fine. All businesses go through downturns. Things will pick up now that it's spring. Not that you'd notice by the weather.'

Jane chewed her lower lip, her finger absently flicking the corner of the paper. 'It's just with my nephew's autism therapy costing so much I couldn't bear to cut back my hours, or worse, to lose this job.'

Holly would rather live on the street than see Jane short of money to fund her young nephew's therapy. She took Jane's hand. 'You are *not* going to lose your job. I can't run this place without you.' She let her assistant's hand go to pick up her secateurs. 'Anyway, I hear divorce parties are big business these days.'

'But weddings are your speciality,' Jane said. 'You love everything to do with weddings. Everyone knows that. Do you think it's because you're so anti-men?'

'What's that got to do with anything?'

'You've not exactly made it a secret you think all men are bastards,' Jane said. 'A few of those social media posts of yours have been a little negative and you haven't had a date in what…two and a half years? What if that's putting off potential clients?'

Holly snipped another stem off a rose. 'I hardly see what my opinion of men has to do with running a successful floristry business. I don't need a man in my life. I'm fine. *F-I-N-E*. Fine.'

'If you don't get more wedding work, you're finished.' Jane's tone was grim. Funereal grim. 'There are other wedding florists in London, you know. Competition is tough. What you need is an image makeover. Or a man. Or both.'

Holly put her secateurs down. 'What is this obsession with finding me a partner? Why does everyone think a woman is lacking something if she hasn't got a man in her life?'

The computer pinged to say another order had come in. Jane moved across to read the screen and sighed. 'There goes another one. The Mackie wedding in June. Cancelled.'

Holly came over and peered at the email, her stomach feeling like she'd ingested thorns. Hundreds and hundreds of prickly thorns. Like the other three cancellations, there was no explanation. Was it *her* fault? Had she been too vocal about her anti-men phase? She straightened from the computer. 'Okay. So maybe I'll shut up on social media about how much I hate two-timing men.'

Jane drummed her fingers on the bench like she was accompanying the cogs of her brain turning over. 'Hey, I have an idea. Get someone to take a photo of you at the divorce party standing next to Zack Knight. Get Kendra to do it. She's got gazillions of followers. A photo of you two flirting with each other would be sure to go viral. Then your problem's solved.'

'Brilliant suggestion, Jane, but as far as I'm concerned flirting is as bad as the other F-word. Anyway, I hung up my flirting boots a long time ago.' Holly picked up the secateurs and wished she had both of her exes handy so she could prune off their most prized parts of their anatomy. 'I don't even know how to do it any more.'

And even if I did, I wouldn't do it.

The divorce party was being held at a swanky hotel in the heart of London. The champagne was flowing like a fountain on fast-forward, but the lively chatter and party atmosphere did nothing to improve Holly's mood. The tiny teeth of panic were nipping at her stomach lining like aphids on rose petals. What if she couldn't meet her financial commitments? What if her business folded?

What if she failed? That was another F-word she hated. *Failure.*

Holly was tucking into her second slice of black forest cheesecake when Zack Knight arrived. She knew it was Zack because of the way the mostly female guests gave a collective gasp of awe when he entered the room. Holly would have gasped too if it hadn't been for the mouthful of cheesecake she'd just spooned in. She could never resist cheesecake. It was her weakness. Well, one of them anyway. She had seen photos of Zack in the gossip pages but had never met him in the flesh. The photos hadn't done him justice. Not one bit of justice. Had she ever seen a more gorgeous-looking man?

He was head and shoulders over everyone in the room, which was saying something because even though most of the women were wearing skyscraper heels, he still towered over them like a thoroughbred stallion surrounded by circus ponies. His jet-black hair was styled in one of those casual, just-got-out-of-bed-after-wild-sex styles that gave him a rakish air. He was clean-shaven but the rich dark pinpricks of stubble had a sexy urgency about them that suggested there was no lack of supply of potent male hormones pulsing through his blood. His skin had an olive tone that glowed with a light tan, which highlighted the healthy vital energy that surrounded him like an aura.

Holly could feel the energy he radiated all the way across the room. It was like his body was sending out a radio signal and hers was sending a response. *Peep. Peep. Peep.* Her skin lifted in a shower of goose bumps, even the backs of her knees tingled and something lying asleep deep and low in her belly woke and stretched its limbs like a languorous cat.

Zack's mouth looked as if it was no stranger to smiling. Not just any old smiling. The sort of smiling that could melt the strongest of feminine willpower like a blowtorch through a block of ice.

His gaze swept the room and suddenly honed in on Holly's. His dark brows rose ever so slightly in a do-I-know-you? fashion that made the sleepy cat in her belly start to purr. She could feel the vibrations inside her body. Deep inside her body, sending hot little flickers of awareness between her thighs. His gaze went to her mouth and then did an assessing sweep of her figure, and another frisson passed over her flesh as if he had reached across the room and touched her.

Holly couldn't understand why her heart was flip-flopping like a frantic fish. Her breathing was shallow and hurried as if she'd run up a flight of stairs. Two flights. Possibly more. Her body felt like it was being heated up from the inside, making her skin hot and tight and so sensitive she became aware of every fibre of her clothing against her body.

She couldn't remember meeting a more attractive-looking man. She might be over men, but even a confirmed celibate like her wasn't completely immune from such an amazing vision of manhood. His body was toned from regular exercise or good genes or both. Or maybe it was from marathon sex sessions with his numerous lovers. Holly could see why women found him irresistible. She was half a room away and could feel his magnetic pull like she was a puny little florist pin and he an industrial-strength magnet.

His gaze came back to hers and his lips curved upwards in a confident smile that did strange things to her pulse and other parts of her anatomy. He crossed the floor towards her. He had a purposeful I-never-fail-to-meet-my-goals gait that more or less confirmed what she knew of him. He was a lethal opponent in a court of law. The word on the street: you engaged Zack Knight's services—expensive as they were—before your ex-partner did. He worked overtime for his clients and, while they paid for it, he always delivered. Always. He acted on some of the dirtiest celebrity divorces in the country and always made sure his clients left court with a fist pump of victory.

Holly only realised she was holding her breath when she became light-headed. Or maybe it was the two glasses of champagne she'd drunk earlier. That was another one of her weaknesses—champagne. The drink of celebrations, even though she had nothing to celebrate and no one with whom to celebrate. Or maybe it was because Zack Knight had come to stand within half a metre of her and every cell in her body was jumping up and down like a hyperactive cheerleader and saying, *Yippee!*

'I believe you're responsible for the flowers tonight.' His voice was a rich baritone, warm honey rolled over gravel. His eyes did a slow appraisal of her and he added, 'Beautiful.'

Holly was so fixated on the startling colour of his eyes she couldn't locate her voice. A smoky blue with flecks of navy in the irises and on the outer rim as if someone had drawn a precise circle around them with a felt-tip marker. She raised her chin a fraction. 'You don't strike me as a man who would stop long enough to smell the roses.'

A glint appeared in his eyes like twin diamond chips and the sound of his laugh rumbled down the entire length of her spine. 'There's nothing I love more than a prickly rose. The thornier the better.'

Holly tried not to look at his mouth but his smile made her think of how it would feel to have those lips move hotly, temptingly, passionately against her own. His lips were more or less evenly sized with well-defined vermillion borders. Firm and yet sensually sculptured and lethally attractive. And this close she could see the way his stubble peppered his jaw and around his nose and mouth. It had been more than two years since she had touched a man's face. She hadn't felt a man's kiss in so long she could barely recall what it was like any more.

Zack held out his hand. 'Zack Knight.'

Holly placed her hand in his and a zap of electric energy shot through her hand and straight to her core, buzzing there like a fizzing sparkler. *Seriously, she had to get out more.* She was acting like a sex-starved spinster, which she was, but still. His hand was warm and dry and large. His fingers closed around hers with the slightest pressure and she couldn't stop thinking what it would feel like to have those strong masculine hands sliding over her flesh, over her breasts, over her belly and below...

'Holly Frost.' She made sure the don't-mess-with-me tone was back in her voice and yet his smile lifted in a mocking slant, as if he knew how hard it was for her to keep from drooling.

Zack's hand released hers first, which annoyed

her because it made her look like she hadn't wanted to let him go, which she hadn't, but that was beside the point. But then she noticed he opened and closed his fingers a couple of times as if her touch had had the same effect on him. Something passed through his gaze—a flicker of surprise or was it intrigue? Either way, Holly couldn't tear her eyes away from him. The citrus and wood fragrance of his aftershave flirted with her senses, the fresh sharpness as intoxicating as his presence. The deep blue of his sharply intelligent gaze only intensified his commanding presence. He was wearing a blue suit that made his eyes seem all the more striking, and the white business shirt with its casually open collar exposed the strong, tanned column of his throat.

'Would you like a drink?' Zack asked.

Holly didn't need any more alcohol. She was tipsy from just looking at him. 'No, thank you. I've had my two drinks for the evening.'

That diamond glint was back in his eyes as if her saying no had secretly delighted him.

'Are you driving?'

'No. I caught a cab.'

'I can't tempt you to break your two-drinks-only rule?'

Holly raised her chin and channelled her childhood Sunday school teacher's prim Temperance Society tone. 'No, Mr Knight. You cannot tempt me.'

Zack's you-just-watch-me smile made something

in Holly's belly flutter like a breeze through the pages of an open book. 'Are you here with anyone?'

'No. I came alone.'

'Is that usual for you?' Something about the tone of his voice made her wonder if they were discussing her relationship status or something much more intimate. Thinking about sex while standing in front of a man as arrantly masculine as Zack Knight was like standing in front of flammable fuel with a lit match.

Dangerous.

Stupidly, recklessly dangerous.

Holly could feel her cheeks heating, her body tingling and her resolve limping away. She stretched her mouth into a stiff no-teeth-showing smile. 'Don't let me keep you from chatting up the other guests.'

'I'm not interested in the other guests. I'm interested in you.' His statement was underlined with determination and his gaze as steady as a marksman's.

Holly mentally gave her resolve a pep talk but it was like trying to get a lame horse to finish a steeplechase. On crutches. 'I can't imagine why you'd be interested in me.' *Damn it.* She sounded like she was flirting.

'Zack!' Kendra Hutchinson came click-clacking towards them in her terrifyingly high heels, her voice so shrill she sounded like a beginner on bagpipes. 'And yay, you've found Holly.' She beamed at Holly. 'I told him *all* about you. I hope you don't mind.'

Holly clenched her teeth behind a polite smile. 'Why should I mind? If Mr Knight is in the market for wedding flowers, then I'm the woman he needs to call.'

Kendra laughed and shone her orthodontist-perfect smile at Zack. 'Isn't she gorgeous? I knew you two would hit it off.'

'Undeniably gorgeous.' Zack's gaze met Holly's, reminding her of a hunter who had just selected his prey.

'Holly hasn't been on a date in two and a half years,' Kendra said to Zack. 'Don't you find that simply amazing?'

What Holly found amazing was how she stopped herself from grabbing one of Kendra's heels, pockmarking her collagen-plumped cheeks with it and taking out a couple of those bright white tooth veneers while she was at it. She might have vented a little ire about men on her Facebook account now and again but she hadn't said anything about how long she'd been celibate. That was no one's business. Who had Kendra been talking to? Jane? Or Sabrina, her best friend, who ran the other arm of Holly's Love Is in the Care business?

'Let's see if I can get her to change her mind about dating,' Zack said with another I've-got-this-nailed smile.

Holly inched up her chin and sent him a haughty glare straight out of a Georgette Heyer novel. 'You'd be wasting your time, Mr Knight.'

'It's my time to waste,' he said.

Kendra took out her phone and held it up to take a picture. 'Smile, you two.'

Holly frowned. 'No. Wait. I don't want my—' Too late. The camera phone flashed and clicked. She could see it now. Hundreds, thousands, possibly millions of social media shares with her standing next to Zack Knight with her mouth hanging open as if she were a starstruck teenage fan at a boy band meet-and-greet.

Kendra checked the photo and smiled like a cat standing beside an empty aviary. She gave Holly and Zack a fingertip wave and turned on her spiky heels to join her other guests.

Holly turned to glower at Zack. 'You should've stopped her. That will be all over Instagram or Twitter in minutes. She'll have us flipping engaged before you know it.'

His shoulder lifted in a nonchalant shrug. 'Who would believe it? I'm not the long-term commitment type.'

Holly wondered why he was so against commitment. Was there some reason behind his date-them-and-dump-them lifestyle? A rejection from a woman in his past that had stung a little too much? Was that why he was happy with hook-up sex but not emotional-connection sex?

Zack took two drinks from a passing waiter and turned back to Holly. 'Still not willing to be tempted?'

She took the glass of champagne, trying not to touch his fingers in the process. If nothing else she could throw it in his face if he got too annoying. 'I'm not the settling-down type either, but I suppose Kendra has already told you that?'

He took a slow sip of his drink and returned his gaze to hers. 'She told me you've had your heart broken a couple of times.'

Argh. Why were people still talking about her doomed love life two and a half years on? It was pathetic. And embarrassing. 'Actually, that's not quite correct. *Bruised* is the terminology I would've used.'

'Bruises still hurt.'

'Is that the voice of experience or observation?'

He lifted his glass as if toasting an eternal truth. 'It's hard to get to the age of thirty-four without a little collateral damage.'

What had put that cynical gleam in his dark blue gaze? What had made his mouth smile in that mocking way?

'So why family law? Why not commercial, criminal or conveyance?'

His gaze remained game shooter steady. 'Why are you a florist?'

'I love flowers.'

'But why wedding flowers?'

Holly could feel her cheeks heating up when she thought of how wedding-obsessed she had been in the past. Her bedroom walls hadn't been plastered with boy band posters but with bridal ones. She hadn't doodled in class with boys' names but had drawn wedding bouquets instead. 'I might not want to get married any more but that doesn't mean I don't love weddings. They're happy occasions where whole families get together to celebrate the commitment of a couple they know and love. I love being a part of that. Helping the bride choose what she wants, finding out her vision for the special day and making sure it happens. I love seeing the church or garden or wherever they're getting married decked out with my designs. And the thought of the bride carrying a bouquet I've made specially for her is very rewarding, and no, I don't just mean financially.' Holly stopped to draw a breath and suddenly realised how much she had told him. And what a good listener he was. 'But you didn't answer my question. Why family law?'

'It pays the bills.'

Holly flicked her gaze over his superb tailoring. 'Apparently quite handsomely too.'

Zack's lazy smile made something in her stomach flip. Damn the man for being so attractive. 'The golden rule in making a success of your career is never to undersell yourself. If you're good at what you do, then your fees should reflect that expertise.'

'Isn't there a fine line between charging a fee for a service and exploiting people during a vulnerable time?' Holly raised her eyebrows and injected her tone with Sunday school–teacher disapproval.

He glanced at her mouth, then back to her gaze, his eyes going a deeper shade of blue. Sapphires with a backdrop of steel. 'I don't exploit my clients. I give them what they pay for—excellent service.'

Holly gave him one of her mortuary-slab smiles. 'If ever I find myself in need of a divorce, then you're apparently my go-to man.'

His eyes glinted and her stomach did another jerky somersault. 'Likewise for wedding flowers.'

You're flirting with him.

No, I'm not.

Yes, you are. And you're loving it.

Holly took a sip of her champagne. 'Don't let me keep you.'

'From?'

She waved a hand at the crowd of guests. 'Hooking up with someone for a raunchy one-night stand.'

The glint of amusement was back in his eyes. 'You don't approve of raunchy one-night stands, Miss Frost?'

Holly's cheeks were getting so hot she was worried all her fresh flower arrangements would wilt. Her fault for mentioning raunchy sex, but still. She had trouble thinking of anything *but* sex when standing near him. It was like her mind was stuck in a groove like a vinyl record under a turntable needle. *Sex. Sex. Sex.* She couldn't look at his mouth without thinking of it clamped to hers. She couldn't glance at his hands without imagining them touching her body.

She couldn't look at his body without wanting him to pin her to the nearest surface and have his wild and wicked way with her.

She didn't understand why she was reacting like this. It was out of character. It was like a fever had taken over her body—a virulent fever that sabotaged her self-control like a lightning strike to a power box. She hadn't thought about sex for years. She'd been as celibate as a ninety-nine-year-old nun. But one glance at Zack Knight was enough to make her eggs pack their bags and head for the nearest exit.

Holly forced herself to hold his satirical I'm-going-to-win-this gaze. 'I'm not sure why I'm the lucky recipient of your peacock-like display of charm. And I apologise if this inflicts any bruises to your undoubtedly robustly healthy ego, but I'm not interested in continuing this discussion. Do I make myself unmistakably clear?'

He gave a mock shudder. 'I love it when a woman talks starchy schoolmistress with me.'

Holly's mouth twitched and she hated him for making her smile. She refused to be charmed by him. By any man. 'You're impossible. I've never met a more annoying man.'

'And I've never met a more fascinating woman.'

'Because I'm the only woman who's ever resisted you?'

'So far.' His smile and his tone had a hint of ruthless hunter meets cornered prey.

Holly chastised herself for being so transparent. What was she these days? Cling film? 'I can assure you, Mr Knight, I have zero interest in you physically.' She tried to keep her gaze away from his mouth. Tried, but failed.

He gave a deep chuckle and raised his glass to hers. 'I'll be seeing you. *Ciao.*'

Holly was still thinking of a pithy comeback when he turned and walked away. She stood silently fuming that he'd had the last word. Furious that he'd made her feel things she didn't want to feel. She felt alive for the first time in two and a half years. She was furious because *he* had done that to her. Her blood zinged through her veins like it had been injected with a potent drug.

Holly sucked in a deep breath and marshalled her self-control back on duty. Zack Knight could be as charming and handsome and amusing as he liked— she was not going to break her man drought.

Zack half listened to the conversation going on around him while he watched Holly move about the room. He could tell she was pretending to be captivated by the lively chatter, and every now and again would give a brief smile, but then she'd look vacant.

He couldn't remember a time when he'd been more intrigued by a woman. Kendra had warned him about Holly's self-imposed celibacy. His interest had been piqued because he hadn't had a woman brush him off since he was a teenager. Her cool reception of him turned him on. Dating had become so predictably boring. He figured it was time to change things up.

And right now he wanted Miss Holly Frost with her damn-you-to-hell brown eyes. Eyes so rich a brown they reminded him of toffee. Her eyelashes were thick and ink black like miniature fans. He couldn't stop thinking about her curly, burnished-copper-coloured hair spread over his pillow. Or over his chest. He'd caught a whiff of her fresh flowery scent when he'd stood in front of her and had longed to lean in to breathe in more of her intoxicating fragrance. Her mouth was soft and supple, except when it was flinging quick-witted comebacks at him.

But those lushly shaped lips never failed to draw his eyes, even when they were as flat and as intractable as a search warrant. He couldn't stop looking at her mouth, imagining it crushed beneath his own. Her figure was slim with curves in all the right places, and he couldn't wait to explore those tempting places with his hands, lips and tongue. Her skin was as creamy as a cultured pearl, the only blemish a small dusting of freckles across the bridge of her retroussé nose.

Zack caught her eye from across the room and her mouth flattened, her chin came up and her eyes flashed like sheet lightning. But then her tongue swept over her mouth, her gaze dipping to his mouth and her slim white throat rose and fell in a swallow.

Yep. All the signs were there. He'd been in the game long enough to recognise female attraction when he saw it. It wasn't a matter of blindsided male ego. He could feel the chemistry between them as soon as their hands had touched. The tingling bolt of electricity had jolted him straight to the groin. He could still feel the soft brush of her fingers against his hand. He could still feel the thrum of his blood surging through his veins. Her touch had sent a rocket blast of lust through his flesh that even now rumbled in his body like distant thunder. He'd seen the way she'd kept looking at his mouth, the way her eyes had darkened to pools of simmering desire.

He was prepared to wait. He knew more than most that some of the best things in life were worth waiting for. Holly's little cat-and-mouse game was amusing but he knew it wouldn't be long before she was in his bed.

And that was *exactly* where he wanted her.

CHAPTER TWO

HOLLY WAS NORMALLY the first of her staff at work in the morning but her elderly landlady, Mrs Fry, delayed her. She'd insisted on telling Holly about the other neighbour on the left, who hadn't put the rubbish bins the right distance apart for collection. Behind her back, Holly called her Mrs Pry because nothing escaped the old busybody's attention.

Holly was only renting the small one-bedroom flat while her new home was being renovated. It was taking longer and costing way more than she'd planned, but she knew it would be worth it in the end. Owning her own home was something she'd longed to do ever since she'd moved to London. All those years of living in bedsits or cramped flats where the walls were as thin as cardboard had made her long for her own place. A place she could decorate to her taste, where she could have a pet—a dog because they were so loving and faithful, unlike men.

When Holly arrived at work, Jane turned the computer screen so Holly could see the order that had come in first thing. 'You must have made a good impression on Zack Knight last night. He's ordered flowers for his legal practice. A regular order too. Two dozen roses, a different colour every week.'

Holly leaned forward to glance at the order, her heart doing a little skip and trip when she saw his name. She straightened and hoped her cheeks were not glowing as hot as they felt. 'I don't want his business. I loathed him on sight. He's an egotistical jerk who thinks he only has to smile at a woman to get her into bed.'

Jane's eyes danced so much they could have won a dancing competition. 'And that's not all.' She pointed to the bottom of the order, where it asked for special delivery instructions. 'He wants you to deliver them in person.'

Holly pinched her lips together. 'I'm not a courier, for pity's sake. I'm the owner of this business. I haven't got time to hand deliver roses.'

'His practice is walking distance from here. And if you don't deliver them, then he says here he'll come and get them.' Jane's smile was sugar sweet. 'Won't that be fun?'

Holly snatched up her apron and tied it around her waist with savage movements. 'I'm not kowtowing to that man's outrageous demands.'

'Maybe he likes you. I mean *really* likes you.' Jane

had gone all dreamy looking. 'How cool would it be to be wooed and won by a man as gorgeous as him?'

'You've been watching way too much TV,' Holly said. 'I don't want to be wooed or won by anyone and particularly not by someone who doesn't understand the word *no*.'

'Think about it, Holly.' Jane suddenly turned serious. 'His interest in you could be really good for business. Did you get a photo with him? I've been checking social media but nothing's come up.'

'Kendra took one but she must have changed her mind about uploading it.' *Thank God.*

'I can see the headlines now.' Jane swept her hand from left to right as if to highlight a billboard. '"Top Celebrity Divorce Lawyer Falls for Wedding Florist".' Her grin widened. 'You'll have brides queuing down the footpath once they hear you've caught the interest of London's most eligible playboy.'

Holly rolled her eyes like marbles but her brain was already doing the calculations. How long would a so-called relationship with Zack take to turn her business back around? If spurious gossip had already soured things for her, then why shouldn't she use more gossip to turn things around?

Because dating Zack Knight would be dangerous.

Capital *D* Dangerous.

Holly was finishing an arrangement for a new mother in hospital when the bell on the front door tinkled as someone came in. Normally Jane or one of her other assistants handled customers when she was working on an arrangement. But all three girls were currently out of the shop—Jane on a coffee break and Taylor and Leanne both away sick with colds. Holly put the arrangement to one side and came out of the workroom to the shopfront. She saw Zack Knight standing there with a lazy smile and her breath caught.

She stayed behind the shop counter, gripping it with her hands and setting her shoulders. 'Can I help you?'

'Did you get my order?' His deep blue eyes were backlit with amusement. Or was it mockery?

Holly forced herself to hold his gaze. 'I don't take orders from customers… I mean, specific orders like the one you sent. If you want my roses or any other flowers, you'll have to accept they'll be delivered by my courier.'

'I'll pay you double to deliver them in person.'

Had he somehow heard about her financial troubles? Had everyone? She would *not* fail. She could *not* fail. Holly fixed him with a steely glare and gripped the counter so hard she thought her knuckles would burst out of her skin. 'Mr Knight, I might not have quite the disgusting amount of wealth you've accumulated, but let me assure you I am not in such dire financial straits that I would ever consent to accepting a bribe from you.'

He stepped closer, so close she could smell the sharp citrus scent of his aftershave and the lighter, more subtle fragrance of cleanly showered man. So close she could feel her resolve downing tools and walking off the job. 'Forget about the roses. Have dinner with me instead.' It was a demand, not a request, delivered in a low, deep burr that did strange tickly things to her insides.

Something at the back of her knees fizzed as his lips curved around a smile. She swallowed. Swallowed again. Her heart skipping like it was in a jump rope competition. She was tempted to accept. Tempted because she hadn't been on a date for so long and she was tired of sitting alone in her flat. Tempted because she wanted to prove she wasn't the pushover he thought her to be. It would be fun teaching him a lesson. The sort of fun she hadn't had in a long time. She would have dinner with him and show him he couldn't win her over with his polished charm. And if anyone saw them out and about, the gossip would bring back the brides to her shop.

Holly released her clawlike grip on the counter and let out a you-win-this-round sigh. 'All right. I'll have dinner with you. Tell me where and when and I'll meet you there.'

His smile never faltered but a glint of cynicism appeared in his gaze. 'I have a rule when I date a woman. I pick her up and I deliver her safely home.'

Holly pursed her lips, wondering what her landlady Mrs Fry would make of the handsome celebrity divorce lawyer coming to pick her up. 'I have a rule, as well. Just dinner. Nothing else. Understood?'

'Just dinner.' His gaze locked on hers and something tightly knotted in her belly slowly unravelled. 'I'll look forward to it.' He took out his phone, asked for her number and address and typed it into his contacts. He slipped his phone back into his jacket pocket and gave her another bone-melting smile. 'See you at seven.'

Zack had a couple of mediation meetings to attend and a stack of paperwork so high it rivalled The Shard, the tallest building in London. He sat back in his office chair and tipped his pen back and forth between his fingers, wondering again why Holly had finally agreed to a dinner date. She'd been so adamant about having nothing to do with him. He would like to put it down to his powers of persuasion but he suspected there was some other reason for her capitulation.

She had something to prove, but then so did he.

He wanted her.

He couldn't remember when he'd ever been so turned on by the prospect of a dinner date, much less anything else that might follow. Holly was frosty and feisty, but he would soon melt through her defences. Miss Frost would be Miss Firebrand by the time he was done. He could see it in her eyes—the flash and spark of desire that made him want her all the more.

She was the most captivating challenge he'd encountered in a long time—perhaps ever. When was the last time a woman had stood up to him? It was almost boring these days how easy it had become to select one from the crowd. He found it strangely exhilarating to have to work so hard at changing her mind. Especially when he knew it was herself she was fighting, not him.

His phone rang and when he saw his father's number come up on the screen, his stomach did its usual clench. His father had never got over Zack's mother leaving him for another man when Zack was ten years old. Twenty-four years had passed and his dad was still hoping Zack's mum would come back. He'd had a few relationships since, but they always followed a predictable pattern—the honeymoon phase and then the hell-on-earth phase. His dad was currently in the hell phase, having broken up with his partner a few months ago. His dad didn't cope well with rejection. It could take months for him to get his life back on track, with a lot of help from Zack. And then it would all start again when his dad got involved with someone else.

Zack had seen it professionally too many times to count. Men or women who couldn't let go of a love they had lost. And how the old pain of unresolved issues poisoned every other relationship.

It made him all the more determined never to fall in love. He didn't want to be one of those people, the broken-hearted person who couldn't function any more without their partner. To this day his dad still struggled to hold down a full-time job after a break-up.

How could loving someone be worth all that suffering?

He tossed his pen onto his desk and picked up the phone. 'Hi, Dad, how are things?'

'I'm okay...' His voice was flat and toneless and Zack wondered if he had been drinking again. *Please, God. No.*

'Just wondered what you were doing this evening. Thought we could hang out. Grab a meal, watch a movie or take in a show or something.'

Damn. Zack rubbed a hand down his face. He'd forgotten today was his parents' wedding anniversary. The first of April was always a bad day for his dad. It wasn't called April Fool's Day for nothing. It was marginally better if his dad was in a relationship but his recent break-up had made his dad depressed. Zack usually kept his diary free so he could take him out and distract him but it had slipped his mind for some reason. Should he tell his dad he already had a date?

But how could he?

If he left his dad to his own devices, who knew what might happen? His dad had been sober for months but Zack knew from experience that he was always only one drink away from a binge. Anniversaries, Christmas and birthdays were the days he had to take action to make sure his dad was safe—or at least as safe as he could keep him, especially when his dad was in a single-and-hating-it phase.

'If you're too busy…'

'No. I'll make it work.' Zack injected a shot of enthusiasm in his voice. 'I'll pick you up at seven.'

He ended the call and pulled up Holly's number on his phone. He sat staring at it for a long moment. There were few people in his life who knew about his dad's struggles and he wasn't about to start sharing now. He'd spent most of his life watching out for his father and he didn't need anyone to know how hard it could be at times.

It wouldn't change anything—it never did.

He pressed the call button but it went through to voicemail. He felt a stab of disappointment. He left a brief message and clicked off his phone. Under normal circumstances he would have sent flowers by way of apology, but sending flowers to a florist seemed a bit weird. He ordered some specialist chocolates instead and sent them by courier with instructions to pick up his handwritten note from his office first. He knew Holly had a sweet tooth because he'd seen her at the dessert table at the divorce party. He smiled at the memory of her spooning gooey black forest cheesecake into her kissable mouth.

Yep, Holly Frost was definitely worth the work and the wait.

* * *

Holly was in a Love Is in the Care late-afternoon business meeting with Sabrina. They met at least once a week for coffee or dinner or drinks after work when their schedules obliged and caught up on industry gossip and any issues to do with their businesses. If it was a coffee and quick catch-up, they took turns to meet in each other's work premises and today it was at Sabrina's studio, a few roads away from Holly's shop.

'Has business picked up at all?' Sabrina asked, passing a slice of carrot cake Holly's way.

Holly held up her hand. 'Not for me. I had two helpings of cheesecake at Kendra's party last night. And no, business hasn't improved. I had another cancellation yesterday.'

'Oh, no! Not another one?'

'I don't know what's going on. Normally at this time of year I have a full diary of weddings. Why aren't I getting business any more? Now I have to resort to doing divorce parties.'

'So how was your first divorce party?'

'Interesting.' Holly eyed the carrot cake. 'I met Zack Knight. He did Kendra's divorce for her. She took a photo of Zack and me standing together. I've been dreading her uploading it on social media, but so far she hasn't, which kind of makes me even more nervous. You know Kendra. She fancies herself a matchmaker.'

'I saw a photo of Zack recently in a gossip magazine,' Sabrina said. 'What's he like in person? He looks gorgeous. Is he even better-looking in the flesh?'

Holly could feel her cheeks betraying her. *Darn it.* She couldn't even hear his name without blushing. And the less she thought about his flesh the better. 'He was exactly as I expected him to be. Full of charm and full of ego.'

Sabrina's expression was so full of intrigue she could have moonlighted as a gossip hound. 'And?'

'And…I'm going out to dinner with him this evening.'

'You're what?' Sabrina's eyes went as round as the cake plate. 'But I thought you said you never wanted to—'

'It's just dinner.' Holly picked a crumb of carrot cake off the plate. Crumbs were another one of her weaknesses. 'I'm only going so I can teach him a lesson. He thinks he can wine and dine me and then I'll automatically fall into his bed. I'm going to show him there is one woman left on the planet who is immune to him.'

'I don't know, Holly. You might be taking on more than you can handle with someone like him.'

'I'll be fine.' Holly licked some cream cheese icing off her fingers. 'I know what I'm doing. Besides, it will be good for my reputation to be seen out and about with a man. Jane thinks I'm to blame for the cancellations for venting my spleen about men on social media.'

'You have been rather negative. That can really damage your brand.' Sabrina chewed her lower lip. '*Our* brand.'

Something in Holly's stomach fell off a shelf. 'Have *you* had cancellations for wedding dresses?'

'Only one.'

'Only one?' Holly leaned forward. 'When did they cancel? Did they give a reason? Who was it?'

'The Mackie wedding.'

Holly was horrified that anything she had done or said was affecting her best friend's business. Maybe Jane was right. She needed an image makeover. She needed a man. 'I'm so sorry. I had no idea my venting would hurt you.'

'It might not have anything to do with you.'

'But what if it does?' Holly asked. 'I need to get into damage control. As soon as possible.' She wiped her sticky fingers on a napkin and then picked up her phone to check the time. She saw that while it had been on Silent a call had come in. She didn't recognise the number but the caller had left a message on her voicemail.

'Excuse me for a sec,' Holly said. The message was brief and from Zack. She was so busy listening to the deep and sexy timbre of his voice that it took her a moment to realise he was cancelling their dinner date. Disappointment trickled through her like iced water. Why had he cancelled? Had he got a better offer? Someone far more enthusiastic about going on a date with him? Someone more beautiful? More glamorous and sophisticated?

Someone who would put out?

Holly clicked the off button and tossed the phone back in her bag.

Sabrina leaned closer. 'Why are you frowning like that?'

'Apparently Zack has overlooked a prior engagement.'

'He cancelled?'

Holly sighed and picked up the carrot cake. 'I've been stood up. Story of my life.' She glanced at Sabrina mid-mouthful of cake. 'What are you doing tonight? Do you fancy dinner and a movie?'

'I've got an even better idea.' Sabrina leaned down and dug out a West End flyer from her tote bag. 'One of my clients has a sister who is an actor in a musical in the West End. I'll call her and see if I can get a couple of last-minute tickets. We can dress up and have a girls' night out. Sound good?'

'Sounds perfect.'

Zack rarely enjoyed a night out with his father. He felt more like a guardian than a son. Not that his dad couldn't be good company at times, but this day in April was never a good day on the William Knight calendar. After a ridiculously expensive dinner where his dad talked at length about how lonely he was, Zack was ready to turn to drink himself. He'd managed to get some good seats for a West End show. He'd figured a movie, especially the sad one his dad had mentioned in passing, was not going to do anything to improve his dad's mood. The musical wasn't to Zack's taste but he was prepared to get his dad through the evening no matter what.

But, upbeat musical or not, as the evening went on his dad became more and more maudlin. He sank lower and lower into his seat and, even though the music was loud, Zack could still hear his father sigh with depressing regularity.

Zack tried not to think of the night he could have been having with Holly. During the interval, he did his best to listen while his dad went through every reason why his life sucked since his divorce twenty-four years ago.

The musical finished close to eleven p.m. Zack waited in the theatre foyer while his dad went to use the bathroom. He scrolled through his messages and found a curt text from Holly. He'd offered her a rain check and she'd texted back.

No, thanks.

Zack was surprised at how disappointed he was. Surprised and galvanised. He would have to work harder to win her over. He smiled to himself and put his phone back in his pocket. But then he saw Holly not more than a metre or two away, coming out of the other side of the theatre with a young woman. The dark-haired woman was attractive, but he only had eyes for Holly. Her emerald-green dress was sweater girl snug against her breasts and clung to her shapely hips and thighs as if spray-painted to her body. Her black high heels had little straps that wrapped around her dainty dancer ankles. Ankles he wanted wrapped around his waist. With her curly copper-coloured hair in a sophisticated up-do and cover-girl make-up, she was sweet girl next door meets sexy supermodel. She laughed at something her friend said and something in his chest gathered together like the final stitch in a wound. The tension trickled down to his groin, hot, tight, tempting. He was vaguely conscious of his breath stopping and starting like the stutter of an old engine.

Rein it in, buddy. But right then his brain wasn't listening to his body.

Holly suddenly turned her head and registered him standing there and her gaze narrowed and heated to a fulminating glare. Her fingers tightened on her clutch purse and then she came striding towards him, weaving through the knot of theatregoers.

'Enjoying your *prior engagement*, Mr Knight?' Her words cut through the air like shards of ice and she looked to either side of him, presumably to locate his date.

Under normal circumstances, Zack would never have explained he was on a night out with his father. But he felt Holly deserved some explanation. A city this size and they happened to choose the same West End show? *Give me a break.* 'I'm sorry about cancelling tonight. I forgot I promised my father we'd spend the evening together.'

Her expression faltered for a moment. 'Your... father?'

'Yes. He's just gone back to use the bathroom.' Zack nodded towards the direction of the theatre toilets. 'He'll be out soon.'

'How soon?' A note of cynicism sharpened her tone another notch.

Zack glanced at Holly's friend, who was watching them from a distance, her expression reminding him of a spectator at a boxing match. So far he was losing. Big time. He turned his attention back to Holly. 'There must be a long queue or something.'

'Actually, that would be the female toilets with the long queue.' Holly's eyes flashed. 'I don't suppose your...erm...*father* is using one of those?'

His father was taking so long to come out Zack was starting to worry. Surely it didn't take this long to take a leak? Could his father have taken a back exit? Was he even now downing a few drinks at a nearby pub? Drowning his sorrows in a glass of whisky? Multiple glasses of whisky? His mouth clamped to a barrel of the stuff? 'Holly, I can explain—'

'Please don't waste your breath or my time.' Holly's chin came up and a bomb went off behind her eyes. Shrapnel and scorn rained down on him.

Should he tell her about his concerns about his dad? He had told no one. It was too private. Too personal. Too painful.

Zack's guts churned at the thought of having to search every pub in the neighbourhood. Of finding his dad sitting in a dark corner, quietly sobbing into his scotch, like so many times before. So far he'd kept the press away from his private life, but since his dad had moved back to London from the West Country a couple of months ago after this recent break-up, he wondered, how soon before someone connected him with the sad drunk who couldn't get his life back on track? Not that Zack was ashamed of his father—he felt sorry for him more than anything. Sorry for him and frustrated with him at the same time. But he knew if the press brought attention to his father, it would only push his dad further into a pit of despair, perhaps even push him over the edge...

Zack released a slow breath, hoping it would calm his racing pulse and spiralling panic about his father's whereabouts. 'My father is going through a rough time just now and I—'

'My heart bleeds.' The sarcasm in her tone stung like a slap. She walked back to her friend, and a section of Holly's up-do fell from its position and swung from side to side as if it too were giving him the flick.

Zack was torn between wanting to go after her and the need to find his father. He couldn't risk it. Not today of all days. This time his father had won.

But didn't he always?

'That was Zack Knight, wasn't it?' Sabrina asked. 'What did you say to him? You looked like you were going to hit him.'

'Drat that odious man.' Holly grabbed Sabrina's arm and led her out to the street. 'This is exactly why I've stopped dating. He said he was here with his father. His father! Who takes their father to a musical? Excuse me while I throw up. Does he think I'm that naïve?'

'Not all men are two-timing jerks. Maybe he really was here with his father. Or his mother.'

Holly gave her the side-eye. 'Or his sister? His second cousin twice removed who happens to be his personal trainer?'

Sabrina grimaced. 'Point taken.'

Holly glanced back to see if Zack's 'father' had joined him but there was no sign of either Zack or whoever was supposedly with him. She'd been a fool to think she could outsmart him. Damn him for turning the tables on her. He was probably on his way back to his palatial penthouse by now with his 'date'. *Grr.* She wished now she'd acted a little more blasé about him cancelling their date. Why should she care if he decided to take someone else out? She hadn't wanted to go out with him in the first place. Of course she hadn't. Well…maybe just a wee bit.

'He's amazingly handsome, isn't he?' Sabrina's voice had a note of star-struck fan about it. 'Like one of those European aftershave models, all brooding and sexy. No wonder you're feeling a little disappointed.'

'I'm not disappointed. I was only going to go out with him to mess with his head. And to improve my reputation. But I'll think of some other way to do that. I will not be jerked around by a man who's a player.' Holly blew out a breath like she was blowing out the last candle on her self-esteem. 'Damn. I wish I'd seen who he was with. I wonder where he was sitting. I'd like to know who my competition is.'

'I'm not sure who could compete with you wearing that dress,' Sabrina said. 'You look amazing.'

Holly tucked her escaping section of hair back into position. 'Humph. I didn't think it was possible to dislike a man so much.' *And still be attracted to him.*

Holly got back to her flat a short time later to find a package had been left on the table outside her door. Mrs Fry always left any post or parcels that came for Holly if she didn't come home straight from work. She picked up the gift-wrapped box with a small card attached and took it inside her flat. She took the card out of its envelope and read the message.

Sorry to cancel at short notice.

Hope these make amends.

Zack Knight

Holly studied the bold strokes of his handwriting for a long moment. She put the card down and un-wrapped the package to find a box of handmade chocolates from a high-street chocolatier. How had he known one of her weaknesses was chocolate?

Holly began to take one out of the box but then snatched her hand away. *No.* She was not going to be tempted. He could send her boxes and boxes of chocolates, truckloads of them, but she was not going to let one past her lips.

Not a single one.

Zack searched four pubs before he found his father. He was sitting at a booth at the back of the pub with a drink clasped between his hands that thankfully looked like it hadn't been touched.

His dad looked up as Zack slid into the booth opposite. 'I know what you're going to say, so don't start. You don't understand. You've never been with someone longer than a week or two.'

'Dad...' Zack moved the whisky out of his fa-ther's reach. 'I know it's hard. It's always been hard for you, but you have to accept that some relation-ships end and you have to move on.'

'Move on?' His dad leaned his elbows on the table

and dropped his head into his hands. 'How can I move on? Every relationship I have ends up failing. It's because I can't love anyone else like I loved your mother. I keep trying but it never works.'

Zack wondered if his dad really did still love his mother or was longing for the life they'd once had. Theirs had been a whirlwind courtship ending in marriage, hastened by his mum becoming pregnant with him. And while the marriage had been mostly happy for the first few years—or maybe he'd been too young to know any better—it hadn't taken long for his mother to look elsewhere for entertainment. Zack's dad had forgiven her for an affair with the gardener, and another with the pool man, but the following year she'd left him for the local vicar, creating an enormous scandal that people in the village still talked about to this day.

Zack put his hand on his father's shoulder. 'It's been twenty-four years, Dad. Surely that's enough time to—'

His dad raised his head to look at him. 'You're as stuck as I am. That's why you don't date anyone long-term. I blame myself for your lack of commitment.'

'I'm happy the way I am. I don't need someone permanent in my life.'

'I tried my best to be a good father but I failed you.'

'You're a great father. Stop being so down on yourself.'

'But you're a *playboy*.' His dad's tone couldn't have sounded more disappointed if he'd said Zack was dealing cocaine.

Zack laughed but somehow it didn't sound too convincing. 'Hey, I thought you admired my life-style.'

'Do you know how it makes me feel? Like a failure. A dismal, pathetic failure. I can't have a success-ful relationship and neither can you. I've cursed you with my own inadequacies.'

Zack was shocked to find his father blamed him-self for his lifestyle. So what if he shied away from commitment? That wasn't an inadequacy—it was his choice. It had nothing to do with his childhood. Well, not much. 'That's crazy, Dad. I don't consider it a failure to be single.'

'You don't understand.' His dad looked at him with a watery gaze. 'Your mother and I had ten years together. Ten years where everything was fine. You haven't been in love. You don't know how wonder-ful it is to be that close to someone. You haven't met The One.'

I hope to God I don't. He didn't want to end up like his father, emotionally shattered by every rela-tionship that came to an end. He didn't want the re-sponsibility of someone else's emotional upkeep. It was hard enough supporting his father for all these years. But he had to do something to ease his fa-ther's guilt. He had to show his father he wasn't the man whore he thought he was. And he knew exactly how to do it. He just had to convince Holly to go out with him.

'Dad, actually there is this girl I've met. She's pretty special. I think you'd approve.'

His dad grabbed Zack's wrist. 'Really? How special?'

'It's early days, but I've never felt this way about anyone else.' It wasn't a lie. Zack had never felt so drawn to a woman before. He only had to picture Holly's flashing gaze and plump mouth and he got hard. Rock-hard.

His father's expression brightened like someone had turned up a dimmer switch. 'It would make me so happy to see you settled with a nice girl. Maybe give me a couple of grandkids—'

'Hey, hold on.' Zack laughed and got to his feet. 'Let's not get ahead of ourselves.' He picked up his dad's coat off the booth seat and handed it to him. 'Come on. Let's get you home.'

CHAPTER THREE

HOLLY HAD TO get up early the next morning in order to get to the New Covent Garden Flower Market, which opened at four a.m. She could have flowers delivered, and often did so when pressed for time, but at least twice a week she liked to select her own, especially when she had a run of weddings. Not that she had any weddings on the horizon, but still. She could dream, couldn't she? The bright array of colours never failed to lift her spirits. Roses in every colour imaginable, pink and white and blue hydrangeas, gorgeous pink and white peonies the size of teacups, sweet william, tall, stately irises in cobalt blue or egg yolk yellow, fragrant lilies and colourful tulips and baby's breath as white as a summer cloud.

She could still remember the first time she'd come to the market. She had stood surrounded by scent and vivid colour, feeling like she was in heaven. Over the years she had got to know some of the vendors and always enjoyed a quick chat as she made her selection.

One of her favourite vendors, Katarina, called out as soon as she saw Holly walking towards her stall. 'Morning, Holly. Loved that post the other day about two-timing men. Couldn't agree more.'

Oh, God. How many of those negative posts had she put out there? Too many if the cancellations in her diary were any indication. Holly's smile was like a crack on concrete. Tight and twisted. 'I guess not all men are like that.'

Katarina gave a half roll of her eyes. 'Yeah, right—only the ones you and I have dated.'

Holly leaned down to smell the creamy pink tea roses on her friend's stall. 'Mmm… These are gorgeous.'

'I can get you more if you need them.'

Holly straightened and sighed. 'I would have taken all of those and more if one of my clients hadn't cancelled their wedding.'

'That's too bad. But another day another bride, as they say in the business.'

'That's what I'm hoping.'

Holly moved on a short time later, but she couldn't help thinking her visits to the market might one day come to an end if she didn't turn her finances around. She made a good profit from cut flowers and other arrangements but it was the wedding business that brought in the bulk of her income. Some clients just wanted bouquets; others wanted the whole shebang—bouquets, flowers for the church and the reception. Nothing thrilled her more than a big wedding project that involved hours and hours of creative work. She couldn't bear the thought of losing the wedding arm of her business. It was her reason for getting out of bed in the morning. It was all she had ever wanted to do—design and create beautiful wedding flowers. Why did life have to be so cruel to threaten to take it away from her?

By the time Holly got back to her shop and unloaded the back of her minivan, Jane had arrived, carrying a coffee for her and a chocolate-chip muffin from their favourite café down the road.

'Here you go.' Jane handed the cup and the muffin to her.

Holly recoiled from the brown paper bag. 'I'll have the coffee but not the muffin. Sorry.'

Jane's eyebrows lifted. 'But you always have a choc-chip muffin on market mornings.'

'I know, but I kind of overdid it with some chocolates last night.' Holly hadn't been able to stop herself from eating half a box of Zack's chocolates… Well, maybe it was two-thirds, which didn't bode well, in her opinion. If she couldn't resist his chocolates, how was she going to resist him if he took it upon himself to ask her out again?

'How did your date with Zack go?' Jane asked.

'He cancelled, but I happened to run into him at the

theatre where I went with Sabrina after our meeting,' Holly said. 'He sent chocolates to my flat by way of compensation. I gave him my address when I agreed to go out with him. Wish I hadn't now.'

Jane frowned. 'Did he have someone with him?'

Holly rolled her eyes. 'He told me he was with his father. That's a new one, I'll give him that. Owen, my first ex, once told me he was visiting his grandmother. I found out later his grandmother had been dead for five years. Peter, my second ex, told me he was spending the night at his cousin's house. He failed to mention the cousin was a distant one twice removed and also his personal trainer.'

'Is that the one he's married to now?'

Argh. Don't remind me. 'Yep. And she's having twins this summer.' Holly huffed out a sigh. 'I'm rubbish at relationships.'

'Don't be so hard on yourself. But did you actually see who was with him last night? I mean, he could've been telling the truth.'

Holly scowled into her coffee. 'Not flipping likely.'

A few days later Kendra came into Holly's shop. 'How are you and Zack getting on?' she asked with a teasing smile. 'Fallen in love with each other yet?'

Holly forced her lips into a be-polite-to-the-customer-who-thinks-she's-my-best-friend smile. 'It turns out he's not that into me after all. He asked me out and then stood me up. He's seeing someone else.'

Kendra frowned. 'But that can't be possible. I know for a fact he hasn't dated anyone for a few weeks now. At least three weeks—maybe even more. He only had eyes for you the whole evening at my party. I've never seen him act that way before. He told me later how much he enjoyed meeting you. He said you were refreshing. Enchanting, yes, that was the word he'd used. I've never seen him so captivated by someone.'

If he was so darn captivated with her, why had he taken someone else to the theatre? Holly picked up a fallen rose petal, scrunched it in her fingers and tossed it in the bin under the counter. 'I wouldn't go out with him if he asked me. Which he has, by the way. He asked for a rain check, but I said thanks, but no, thanks.'

'I think you guys need a little push in the right direction.' Kendra took out her phone and started tapping and smiled a matchmaker-on-a-mission smile. 'It's my bet he'll be in through that door faster than you can say *wedding bouquet*.'

Holly tried to see what Kendra was typing. 'Hey, what are you doing? Is that Twitter? Oh, God. Don't. Is that the photo you took of us? Please don't put it on Twitter. That's a horrible photo of me. I look like a stranded fish.'

Kendra pressed Send and clicked off her phone.

'Done. I've been saving that photo for the right opportunity. But don't worry—I Photoshopped it. You look besotted with him. If nothing else it will boost your business. I heard things aren't going so well for you just now.'

Holly's stomach felt as heavy as a sandbag. 'Where did you hear that?'

'I know Alexandra Mackie. Our mothers play in the same bridge club. I ran into her yesterday and she told me she cancelled her booking with you.'

'Did she say why?'

Kendra somehow managed to look sheepish and sly at the same time. 'I might have shared your man-hating posts a little too often to all my followers. Sorry. But I can turn it around. Watch and learn.'

Holly could hear the sound of Kendra's Twitter feed going crazy. 'What's going on? What are all those Tweets saying?'

Kendra's smile was vulpine. 'Congratulations, Holly. You just got engaged to London's most eligible bachelor.'

Holly stared at her in shock. *Engaged?* Engaged to Zack Knight? Her heart was thumping like it was aiming for a world record. How was she going to face him? 'But won't *he* have something to say about that?'

'He's got a sense of humour.' Kendra shrugged as if dismissing a chipped fingernail. 'And once we tell him what's been happening to your business, he'll be glad to help. He hates any sort of injustice—that's what makes him such a great lawyer.'

'He's a commitment-phobe,' Holly said. 'It's one of the first things he told me. Who's going to believe he's engaged to me? He's not the settling-down type.'

Kendra's smile had a hint of fairy godmother turned to the Other Side. 'You never know—you might be the one woman to change his mind.'

Zack decided to leave it a few days before he contacted Holly again. He figured she would need time to forgive him for reneging on their date. A cooling-off period was always advisable after a confrontation—something he often encouraged his clients to do.

His dad was in a much better headspace and had even talked about joining a gym to get fit and to meet people. Who knew Zack's little white lie could bring about such a rapid change in his dad's attitude? He only hoped it would continue, and that Holly would agree to go out with him, so he could prove to his dad he could stay in a relationship longer than a week or two.

He'd tried ordering more flowers for his office staff but Holly must have blocked his email. He'd picked up his phone to call her when he saw a message from a mate from another law firm.

Since when are you engaged?

He stared at the message, wondering if it was from a wrong number, but his mate's name, Rob, was on the top of the screen. Another message came in from a person at work mentioning something about his 'engagement' announced on Twitter. Zack checked his newsfeed, his eyes widening when he saw the Tweet from Kendra, accompanied by the photo she had taken of him and Holly the other night at the divorce party.

London's favourite wedding florist's third time lucky engagement to celebrity divorce lawyer Zack Knight.

Zack's heart banged like a bell against his breastbone. A warning bell. A what-the-hell-is-going-on? bell. Who had cooked up such a fantastical scheme? Was it Kendra? His scalp prickled, his pulse thumping like someone was coming towards him with a noose. Or had Holly had something to do with this? Was she deliberately setting him up for standing her up the other night? He was all for a bit of fun, but engaged? No way was he going to buy anyone a ring, only to have them screw him over when they fancied someone else.

Not even hot little Holly Frost.

But then he recalled his dad's words about his lifestyle. Maybe there was a way he could work this to his advantage. He wanted Holly and if he had to jump through a few tricky hoops to have her, then so be it. An engagement between them wouldn't be the real deal. He would make that absolutely clear. As far as he was concerned, *commitment* was a curse word he had cut from his vocabulary.

But a temporary 'engagement' could be just the thing to convince his father he wasn't permanently scarred from his parents' divorce and it might just help his dad finally move on with his life. He felt a little uneasy lying to his dad, but he figured it would be forgivable if it made his father feel less guilty about him. He would prove to his dad he wasn't shying away from commitment *and* he would enjoy a fling with the most fascinating woman he'd ever met.

If that wasn't a win-win, he didn't know what was.

Zack walked into Holly's shop later in the day to find her behind the counter, looking at something on the computer. She looked up when the bell on the door tinkled and her smile of greeting faded. 'Oh, it's you. Sorry. I'm just about to close.' Her voice was as arctic as her gaze, taking the temperature of the room down ten degrees.

'Have you heard about our engagement?'

Her cheeks went the same shade of pink as the peonies on display in the window. 'I had nothing to do with that Tweet. Kendra sent it before I could stop her.' She bit her lip. 'I'm sorry if it's embarrassed you. If we ignore it, hopefully it will go away.'

'What if I told you I didn't want it to go away?'

Her big brown eyes rounded. 'What?'

Zack leaned down to smell the vase of roses sitting on the counter. He straightened and gave her a winning smile. 'What if it suited me to be engaged for a while?'

She stood as stiffly as a sunflower stalk. 'It might suit you but it doesn't suit me.'

'You've been engaged before. Two times, wasn't it? What's one more time?'

Her eyes narrowed to hairpin slits and she pointed a rigid finger towards the door. 'Get. Out.'

Zack wasn't easily daunted, especially by someone who so clearly was at war with herself rather than him. *Commitment* might be a word he disliked but the word *challenge* was his all-time favourite. 'I've been trying to order flowers from your website but can't seem to get through. Don't you want the business?'

'I don't want *your* business, Mr Knight. And I don't want your stupid chocolates either.'

'Look, I know we got off to a bad start, but—'

'Did you not hear me?' Her toffee-brown eyes flashed like daggers. 'Please get out of my shop before I call the police.'

Zack blew out a long breath. 'I suppose I deserve that.'

'Yes.' She folded her arms and glared at him. 'You do.'

He glanced at her tightly compressed lips. He'd spent the last seven days dreaming about her mouth, wondering what it would feel like, what it would taste like beneath his own. He'd never been so fixated on a woman before. Was it because she'd rebuffed him? Maybe he was more like his dad than he realised. Scary thought. 'Can I buy some flowers before I go?' He pointed to the glass vase of white and lemon-coloured freesias on the display in the window. 'They look nice.'

Holly's neat eyebrows lifted. 'Are they for your father by any chance?'

'One of my secretaries,' Zack said. 'She's in hospital with pneumonia.'

She chewed one side of her mouth as if deciding whether to process the sale or not. 'Do you want them delivered?'

'No, I'll take them. I promised I'd pop in after work.'

Holly moved from behind the counter like she was approaching a dangerous animal. 'Just the one bunch? Or would you like me to make up a bouquet with a couple more?'

'Whatever you think.' Zack gave a crooked smile. 'You're the expert.'

She gave him the sort of look a hardened sceptic would give a snake oil salesman. She went to the display and took out four bunches of the freesias and took them out the back to her workroom. He watched her from the shopfront as she snipped the stems and arranged the flowers into one bunch, artfully adding a few pieces of greenery and wrapping the bunch into white and scarlet layers of tissue wrap and tying a wide scarlet satin ribbon around it.

She came back out and handed it to him. 'There you go.'

'Beautiful.' Zack didn't even glance at the flowers but kept looking at Holly. Her cheeks were still a soft pink and he wondered if he had ever seen a more naturally gorgeous-looking woman. He knew it was going to take some convincing to get her to pretend to be in a relationship with him, but he wasn't a quitter. He knew she was attracted to him. Knew it in his blood and his bones. Felt it thrumming in the air when their gazes locked. She was fighting it out of pride or a pert desire to put him in his place.

But he would win her over or die of lust trying.

She took his credit card and processed the payment and passed him the receipt. Her fingers brushed his and he felt the same electric tingle shoot up his arm and straight to his groin. She blinked and pulled her hand back and used it to push some strands of her hair back behind her ears, her gaze moving away from his.

There was a silence so intense you could have heard a rose petal drop.

'So what are we going to do about our engagement?' Zack asked.

Holly's slim throat moved up and down as if she were trying to swallow something large and distasteful. 'You have to tell Kendra to retract her Tweet. I tried to but she wouldn't listen. Apparently she shared some of my negative posts about men on social media. She has more followers than stars in the sky. No wonder my business has hit a rough patch recently. I've had four big weddings cancelled for this summer. Kendra has this weird idea she's helping me by setting me up with you but I can do without *that* sort of help.' Her gaze narrowed to an accusing glare. 'Anyway, I thought you said when we first met at her divorce party that no one would believe it if you got engaged. Well, newsflash. Everyone's flipping well believing it.'

'If your business is suffering a low point, then running with our engagement is one way to turn things around.' Zack was a little shocked at how keen he was on going with this engagement charade but he had his own issues to address. Important issues that could no longer be ignored. 'Do you need some help financially to tide you—'

'No.' Pride flashed in her gaze. 'I'm fine.'

Zack drummed his fingers on the counter. 'We'll have to get you a ring.'

Holly reared back from him as if he'd breathed tongues of fire. 'Are you out of your mind? We do not need a ring because we're not engaged.'

'Think about it, Holly.' He locked his gaze on her feisty one. 'This could work for both of us. Your business will get a much-needed boost and I'll improve my reputation as a reformed love-them-and-leave-them playboy. It's a win for both of us.'

She chewed at the side of her mouth, her gaze still sceptical. 'But why do you want to improve your reputation? I thought you weren't the settling-down type?'

'I'm not. But that doesn't mean I can't pretend to be engaged for a while.'

'How long is a while?'

He shrugged. 'Who knows? A few weeks? A few months?'

Her mouth fell open. 'A few *months*?'

He grinned. 'Okay, so maybe that's stretching it a bit, but how long do you think it will take to improve things here?'

She gnawed at her lip again. 'It's April so we usually get bookings steadily from now on for spring and summer next year. Sometimes we get them at short notice for the current year—or at least I hope we will to make up for the four we've lost.' Her forehead creased into another tight frown. 'But you didn't tell me why you're willing to do this. It's not just about your reputation, surely?'

He held her gaze. 'You can't guess?'

She moistened her lips. 'Pretending to be engaged to you doesn't mean I'll sleep with you.'

'But you want to.'

Her cheeks pinked up again. 'I need to think about

this for a day or two. By the way, thank you for the chocolates.'

'I was going to send you flowers, but thought it might be a bit weird.'

She met his gaze, her shoulders dropping on a sigh. 'No one ever buys me flowers and yet they're my favourite thing in the world.'

'Really? No one? Ever?'

She shook her head. 'Nope.'

Zack pointed to the peonies in the window. 'Can I buy five bunches of those?'

'Five?' She stepped from behind the counter, her expression wary.

'They remind me of the colour of your cheeks when I make you blush.'

'I do not blush,' she said and promptly did so. 'Do you want them delivered?'

'No. I'll deliver them myself.'

Holly went back to the workroom and wrapped the peonies in tissue wrap and tied them with a different coloured ribbon this time—a lime-green one. She brought the bunch out to him and laid it on the counter while she processed the transaction. She handed him the receipt and the flowers. 'I hope your secretary feels better soon.'

Zack slipped the receipt into his trouser pocket and picked up the peonies and the freesias. 'Thanks. I'm sure these will cheer her up.' He flashed a smile. 'Have a good evening.'

'Thank you.' She paused for a beat and added with the ghost of a smirk, 'Say hello to your father for me.'

'Maybe I'll introduce you to him one day.' Zack had never introduced any of his lovers to his dad before. There had never been time because he didn't stay with a lover long enough. Nor had he ever wanted to. But he had a feeling his dad would approve of Holly. She had a girl-next-door appeal that was utterly enchanting.

'That would be…interesting.' Her eyes drifted to his mouth and then back to his eyes, the hint of peony pink still glowing in her creamy, soft cheeks. 'Just saying I *did* agree to this charade…would you be willing to come to my sister's engagement party with me?'

Zack read people's faces all the time in his line of work and something about Holly's expression told him there was a lot riding on her request even though it seemed reluctant at first.

'I've never been to an engagement party before.'

'Really?'

He gave a lopsided grin. 'I'm an engagement party virgin. Divorce parties? Well, that's another story.'

Doubt flickered across her features. 'So…will you go with me?'

'Where's it being held?'

'At my parents' house just outside Bath.' She blew out a breath. 'And I apologise in advance for my family. They can be a bit overpowering.'

'I'm sure I'll survive. When is it?'

'Next month.'

'Sure, I'll take you,' Zack said. 'But that means you'll have to attend some functions with me too. Agreed?'

The tip of her tongue swept over her lips. 'Okay…'

'Cool.' Zack thought he'd better leave before he was tempted to lean across the counter and plant a kiss on her beautiful lips.

Man, oh, man, did he have the lust bug bad.

Not long after Zack left her shop, Holly got a phone call from her mother and two of her sisters. They were on a five-way merged call and there was no escaping their interrogation. 'Is it true?' Her mother's voice couldn't have sounded more excited. 'Are you engaged to *the* Zack Knight?'

Holly hated lying to her mother, but she couldn't see any way out of it. She couldn't attend another family gathering without a partner and, since Zack was strangely willing to be her plus-one, she decided to run with the charade for the time being. She had to do something about her business and her sister's engagement party. Two birds, one very handsome and very tempting stone. 'We met through a mutual friend. I know it's very sudden but I've never felt like this before.' That much was true. She had never felt the delicious buzz of electricity his touch evoked from anyone else. 'And I'm sorry you found out about it on Twitter. I didn't realise Kendra would announce it before I'd told my family and close friends.'

'I did wonder why you hadn't told us, but we're so delighted you've found someone, darling,' her mother said. 'I've been so worried about you being so un-happy for so long.'

Unhappy wasn't quite how Holly would have de-scribed herself over the last few years. Pissed off. Cynical. Resentful, maybe. 'Thanks, Mum. I'm re-ally happy. You're going to love Zack.' *There isn't a woman alive who doesn't.*

'You go, girl,' Katie chimed in. 'He's traffic-stopping gorgeous. No wonder you've fallen so quickly. When are you getting married?'

'We're not rushing to get married just yet,' Holly said. 'We want to enjoy each other before we start planning a wedding. Besides, I don't want to steal Belinda's thunder. Her wedding should be the focus for now.' Who knew she was so good at lying? Even *she* was starting to believe she was actually engaged to Zack.

'Aw, thanks, Holly,' Belinda said. 'You're always thinking of others. But don't have a long engage-ment, will you? Not like the other two.'

'Zack's nothing like Peter or Owen,' Katie said. 'You can tell that just by looking at him.'

'I'm thrilled for you, darling,' her mother said. 'You'll be bringing him to Belinda's party next month, won't you? I can't wait to meet him. Dad and I have been so worried about you not meeting anyone and here you are, engaged to London's most eligible bachelor.'

'Yes, well, it has been a bit of a whirlwind but when you know, you know,' Holly said.

'True,' her mother said. 'Which was what worried me about Owen and Peter. I always thought you weren't absolutely sure about either of them. There didn't seem to be the right chemistry between you.'

Holly had been subjected to her mother's views on good chemistry for most of her adult life. Even her father, on occasion, expressed his opinion on the subject. She had always blamed herself for not being a sensual person but, since meeting Zack, she wondered if that was strictly true. Her senses went wild when he was around. He only had to look at her with those ink-blue eyes and she melted. How was she going to resist him when he seemed so determined to seduce her?

Damn it. She wanted to be seduced. She wanted to be wooed and kissed and caressed and pleasured like she'd never been pleasured before. But she was worried if she got involved with him physically it would change the power dynamic between them. She would be just another one of his lovers, someone he got involved with for a short time before he moved on. She had never been a casual dater. It was all or nothing for her. That was why she'd ended up engaged twice to men who, in hindsight, were not the best matches for her.

But was Zack, with his fast-living lifestyle, any better?

Holly had barely ended her call with her mother and sisters when Sabrina came into the shop. 'I just saw this thing on Twitter that said...' She peered at Holly's pink cheeks. 'You're not... *Are* you?'

Holly let out a long breath. 'No, but you have to pretend I am engaged to him. I can't let anyone know it isn't real.'

'But...why?'

'I want to improve my image. To not be known as such a man-hater. It'll be good for business.'

Sabrina opened and closed her mouth. 'I can think of heaps of ways you could do that without pretending to be engaged to a man who only a week ago you said you hated with a passion. Are you nuts? And why would *he* agree to that?'

'I'm not sure but I'm not looking this gift horse in the mouth.' Although she was pretty keen on kissing that mouth. Way too keen.

'Are you sure you know what you're doing, Holly?'

'Stop worrying,' Holly said. 'I've got it in hand. He's agreed to come to Belinda's engagement party with me next month. If nothing else it will ward off my mother's matchmaking attempts.'

'Yes, well, there is that, I suppose.' Sabrina's

brow furrowed. 'I have to suffer the same whenever my parents invite Max Firbank over. I don't know why they insist Max and I would be an ideal match. They've been trying to set us up for years. But neither of us can bear the sight of each other. He thinks I'm immature and disorganised and I think he's a stuck-up control freak.'

Max Firbank had been a constant presence in Sabrina's life, being the godson of her parents and Sabrina being the goddaughter of his. He was a handsome and successful architect and travelled the world designing properties for the equally rich and famous.

Holly gave her friend a teasing smile. 'Sometimes I wonder if you hate Max as much as you make out.'

Sabrina's laugh sounded forced. 'Don't *you* start. I get enough of that from my parents and my brothers.'

'Are they still on at you about choosing wedding dress design instead of medicine?'

'Only every time I see them.' Sabrina sighed. 'That's the trouble with coming from a long line of medicos. They think I'm going to get sick of playing dress-up, as they call it, and go back to university and study medicine. Mind you, if our brides keep cancelling their weddings, I might have to do exactly that.'

Not if Holly could help it.

Holly had only been back at her flat for an hour or so when her doorbell rang. She checked her peephole and found Zack standing there, holding the peonies he'd bought from her earlier. She had wondered at the time if he was going to hand them straight back over the counter to her and had been annoyed at herself for feeling disappointed when he hadn't. She was still trying to get her head around his surprising willingness to run with their 'engagement'. What possible reason could he have for doing so?

Because he wants you any way he can have you.

Holly shivered at the thought. She wanted him any way she could have him too. It scared the hell out of her how much she wanted him. Her body was a traitor. It tingled every time she thought of him. And now, with him standing on her doorstep, her body was so excited it was trembling from head to foot.

She opened the door of her flat at the same time as Mrs Fry, who lived across the hall, opened hers. Holly mentally groaned. The last thing she needed was her nosy landlady to cross-examine Zack. 'It's okay, Mrs Fry. I've got this.'

'Are you a salesman?' Mrs Fry asked Zack, sizing him up and down with her birdlike gaze.

'No. I'm a lawyer,' Zack said.

'Oh…' Mrs Fry's eyes narrowed. 'Is Holly in trouble with the law?'

He gave one of his charming smiles. 'Not as far as I know. I'm a family court lawyer. Holly and I are… engaged.' His slight hesitation over the word made

Holly wonder if he was having second thoughts about their 'engagement'.

Mrs Fry turned her wide-eyed gaze to Holly. 'Is that true?'

Holly wanted to deny it but the thought of her mortgage stopped her. So what if she ran with this charade for a bit? It didn't mean she had to sleep with him. She could keep things platonic, couldn't she? Well, as long as her self-control held, that was. 'Yes, it is.'

Mrs Fry nodded as if that news pleased her. 'It's about time this young lady had a man in her life. She's been living here for months and not had a gentleman caller once. It's not natural, not for a young woman her age. When I was her age I was married with four kids. I was starting to wonder if she was—'

'Will you excuse us, Mrs Fry?' Holly said. 'We want to celebrate our engagement tonight.'

Mrs Fry turned her attention back to Zack. 'I don't normally allow my tenants to have sleepovers, but in your case I'll make an exception. But keep the noise down, okay?' She looked at the peonies he was holding and swung her gaze back to Holly. 'He's definitely a keeper. What girl doesn't love a man who buys her flowers?'

Holly could feel her cheeks sending off enough heat to set off the fire sprinklers. Zack was smiling, his gaze twinkling, which only made her face fire up all the more. She waited until Mrs Fry had gone back to her flat on the other side of the hall before she invited him in. 'Sorry about that,' Holly said once they were inside and the door closed. 'My landlady can be a bit over-the-top.'

Zack looked like he was trying not to laugh. He handed her the peonies. 'For you.'

Holly took the flowers and bent her head to smell their light fragrance. The soft petals brushed her nose like dozens of silk tissues. 'Thank you…but why didn't you give them to me as soon as you bought them?'

His smile was lopsided. 'I thought it might make you appreciate them more if you had to wait for them.'

Holly gave a mock scowl. 'Odious man.'

There was a short silence.

'Erm…would you like a drink or something?' Holly said. 'Please take a seat. I'll just put these in some water.'

He followed her into her tiny kitchen. His head almost brushed the light fitting and even when he sat on one of the two kitchen chairs either side of the narrow table, his legs came out the other side. He was still wearing his business suit, but he'd removed his tie and undone the top three buttons of his shirt, revealing a hint of springy dark chest hair. His late-in-the-day stubble was even more pronounced than it had been a couple of hours ago, and she wondered how it would feel against her skin.

'How long have you been living here?' he asked.

Holly opened the cupboard to find a vase. 'Too long. I'm having renovations done at my new house but they're taking twice as long as I expected.' She put the vase on the bench top. 'And they're costing twice as much.'

'Do you have a move-in date?'

'Not yet.' She sighed and untied the ribbon from around the peonies. 'I just keep paying the bills and praying it won't be too much longer.'

'Your landlady seems nice.'

'Nice?' Holly laughed. 'Mrs Fry means well, but she drives me nuts. I call her Mrs Pry behind her back. She's the biggest gossip about the place and pedantic as anything. She actually measures the distance between the rubbish bins with a ruler and issues you a caution if you're a millimetre out.'

He gave a low, deep chuckle. 'It takes all types, I guess.'

Holly arranged the peonies and set them in the middle of the table. 'Thanks for these.'

'My pleasure.' His eyes held hers in a silent lock that made her heart pick up its pace.

She moistened her lips and rubbed her hands down the front of her thighs. 'So...would you like a glass of wine or tea or juice or—'

He stood and came around to her side of the kitchen, stopping just in front of her. 'Why do I make you so nervous?'

'I—I'm not nervous.' Holly's voice stuttered along with her heartbeat.

He picked up one of her curls and wound it around his finger. 'You have such beautiful hair.'

The slight tether of his finger around her hair made her scalp tingle and her breath catch. 'Thank you...'

He slowly unwound the lock of her hair and tucked it behind her ear. 'I'd really like to kiss you right now but I'm not sure how it would be received.'

Holly glanced at his mouth. Wanting. Wanting. Wanting him to kiss her. Needing it like she needed air. Had she ever wanted a man to kiss her more? 'Why do you want to kiss me?' Her voice was so whisper soft she wondered if he'd even heard it.

His fingertip went on a lazy exploration of her lower lip, sending her sensitive nerves into raptures. Then he went to her top one, tracing it in the same slow, methodical manner. Her lips began to buzz, the need to feel more pressure building, not just on her mouth but also deep within her body.

'I want to know if your mouth is as soft and sexy as it looks.' His voice was low and gravel rough, making her want him even more.

Holly suppressed a shudder of delight at the feel of his finger doing another round of her lips. She could taste his salt on her mouth and wondered if she had enough self-control rostered on duty to stop at one kiss. 'I guess one kiss would be okay...since we're engaged and all.'

A dancing light came on in his eyes. 'So you'll agree to run with this for a while?'

Holly swallowed. 'It looks like I haven't got any choice. Twitter has nothing on Mrs Fry. She'll have spread the news so far and wide by now it would be pointless trying to deny it.' She paused for a beat and added, 'And I told my family.'

'Oh, really?' A slow smile tilted his mouth. 'How did they receive the news? Were they happy for you?'

'Ridiculously happy,' Holly said. 'You'd think I'd told them I'd won a mega-draw lottery or something.'

Zack cradled her face in his hands, his fingers warm and gentle against her cheeks. Who had ever cradled her face before? It made her sway towards him, closing the distance between their bodies until she could feel his chest against hers, his muscular thighs brushing hers. She hadn't been this close to a man in years. Two and a half man-drought years.

But this was nothing like being held by either of her exes.

Zack's touch lit spot fires in her flesh, making her heart race and her blood pound. She watched as his mouth came down towards hers as if in slow motion, every nanosecond he took making her throb and ache all the more.

'Are you sure about this, Holly?'

Of course she wasn't sure. She had already suffered the humiliation of two broken engagements and this one would be her third once it came to its inevitable end. But she had to get through her sister's engagement party, not to mention get her business back on track. A temporary flirtation with the world's sexiest man was too tempting to walk away from. If nothing else it would give her battered self-esteem a much-needed boost. 'I'm sure,' Holly said. 'It's not like I'm promising to marry you for real.'

He gave a soft laugh. 'Glad to hear it.' His gaze went to her mouth and the atmosphere tightened. His lips finally—*Thank You, God!*—touched down and covered hers, softly at first like the brush of an idle feather. But then he came back for more, increasing the pressure as if something carefully restrained inside him had broken loose. His mouth moved with building urgency against hers, his tongue gliding through the seam of her lips to play with hers.

To tangle.

To dance.

To mate.

Holly snaked her arms up around his neck, standing on tiptoe so she could feel the burgeoning rise of his male flesh. Raw primal need flashed through her body, a tight ache that was concentrated deep in her feminine core. Every fibre of her being went into raptures as his mouth moved with increasing urgency against hers. She kissed him back as if this was the last kiss she would ever have, her tongue duelling with his in a cat-and-mouse caper that made her blood tick and her heart trip with excitement.

His teeth grazed her bottom lip, and then he took it between them in a soft nip that made the base of her spine tingle. Need rushed through her, a desperate clawing need that made her wonder if she was going to be able to control her response to him. Her body was out of control. Way out of control. Expressing wants and urges she hadn't realised she'd had— her inner core contracting, pulsing with longing, her legs shaky with the effort of standing upright.

A shiver coursed down her spine as his teeth nipped her lower lip again, the gentle sweep of his tongue following. She made a whimpering sound and softly bit his lip, stroking her tongue over it as he had done to hers. She drew his lip into her mouth, sucking on it, teasing it with the flicker of her tongue, mimicking the most intimate caress a woman could do to a man.

His mouth came down on hers, firmer this time, his tongue driving into her mouth with heart-stopping expertise. There was a thrilling familiarity about his kiss as if they had kissed in a past life and finally found each other again. There was no bumping of teeth, no awkward head positioning, no excess saliva or stale breath. He tasted familiar and strange…like something exotic she hadn't realised until now was her favourite flavour. It was a magical meeting of mouths, of lips and tongues and a spiralling need to get closer. She couldn't get enough of him, the glide of his tongue making her senses soar, her heart stammer and her self-control throw its hands up in defeat.

His hands went to her hips and brought her up against his hard body. She could feel the proud jut of his erection and wondered if he could sense how turned on she was. She had never felt desire like it. Her body was on fire, trembling with need. She made a sound against his lips—part whimper, part gasp, part prayer for him to continue.

His hands tightened on her hips, his mouth moving from hers to trail a blazing pathway of heat against the sensitive skin of her neck. Had anyone ever kissed her there? Just below her ear where it seemed every nerve in her body had gathered? Sensations rippled through her flesh, making her aware of every point of contact with his body. Her pelvis was on fire, her feminine mound aching inside with the need for his possession. She could feel the intimate swelling and moistening of her body, the signal of high arousal she had never felt from just a kiss before. She'd barely felt it during what little foreplay her exes had bothered to give her. Was it possible to come from just a kiss? She could feel the pressure building in her body, an exquisite pressure she had never felt before with such bone-melting intensity.

Zack's mouth moved lower, discovering her collarbone. Who knew her collarbone was an erogenous zone? Before his mouth had found it, it had just been her collarbone. Now it was a hive of fizzing sensations as his lips and tongue moved along its length and she couldn't help thinking of what it would be like to do the same to him, but not on his collarbone. She had resisted being so intimate with her exes even though they had pleaded with her. But suddenly she could imagine doing it with Zack. Running her tongue along his hardened length the way he was doing to her.

'You smell beautiful,' he said, so close she could feel the movement of his lips against her skin. 'Like spring flowers.'

'Erm...I'm a florist?'

She felt him smile against her mouth. 'I should stop kissing you.'

'Why should you?' *Had she just said that?*

He lifted his head to meet her gaze, his eyes dark and lustrous with desire. 'You don't want me to stop?'

Holly shrugged as if she didn't care either way. 'It's been a while since I kissed a guy. And we're just kissing, right?'

His gaze went to her mouth. 'It feels like more but maybe that's just me.'

'You're a good kisser.' She flicked her tongue over her lips, tasting him. Missing him. Wanting him. 'I can see why women are falling over themselves to get into bed with you.'

His hands came back up to cradle her face, his eyes meshing with hers. 'I want you but you know that, don't you?'

She sucked in a ragged breath. She wanted him too. So much it hurt. But she had to resist him. She couldn't be the pushover he thought she was. She had backbone, sure she did. She just had to find it. 'Sometimes we can't have the things we want.'

A devilish glint appeared in his eyes. 'You want me.'

Holly pulled out of his hold and put some distance between them—not an easy task in a kitchen as small as hers. She was aware of him in every cell of her body. *Damn it.* Every cell of her body was calling out to him to ignore her last statement and pull her back into his arms and kiss her like he had done before. 'I'm not interested in getting involved with someone right now. I have other priorities.' She looked up to meet his gaze but instead of the how-could-you-lead-me-on? glare she was expecting, she saw compassion.

'What happened between you and your fiancés?'

Holly grimaced. So he, like every other person in the country, knew about her not one but two failed engagements. *Oh, joy.* 'Both of them bailed before the wedding at the last minute. One the week before, the other the day before.'

'Ouch.' He winced in empathy. 'That would've hurt.'

'Not just emotionally, but financially.' She whooshed out a sigh. 'Neither of them were prepared to help out with the costs and I was so fed up with them I didn't push it.'

'So you've been single ever since?'

'Yep. And loving it.' Holly leaned back against the kitchen counter and folded her arms. 'Trouble is, my family thinks I'm missing out. My three sisters are all either married or about to be. My parents have been happily married for thirty-three years and can't bear the thought of me being left on the shelf. That's why my youngest sister's engagement party next month is such a big deal for me. I've been dreading it ever since she sent me the invitation.'

'Aren't you happy for her?'

Holly unlocked her arms and gave him are-you-for-real? look. 'Of course I am, but if I go without a partner, my mother will take it upon herself to find me one. She's a hopeless matchmaker. Even worse than Kendra. Which is basically why I've agreed to pretend to be engaged to you. I feel bad about all the lies I've told my family, but I can't go to that damn party without a partner.'

There was a pulsing silence.

Holly couldn't stop staring at his mouth, reliving every moment of his kiss. Her lips were still tingling from the sensual pressure of his and she could still taste him—the hint of mint and salt that made her want him to kiss her all over again. She waved a hand in the direction of the fridge. 'Erm…would you like a drink or something?'

His gaze was studying her mouth just as she had been doing his. Was he too remembering every moment of their kiss? Wanting more? Aching for more?

His eyes came back to hers and a lazy smile tilted his mouth. 'If I told you what I want right now, you'd probably slap my face.'

Holly's insides quivered with longing and she wondered if he could tell how hard it was for her to resist him. But of course he could tell. No woman had ever resisted him. That was why he was making her his latest mission—because she'd rebuffed his advances. 'I must seem quite a novelty to you.'

Another frown flickered across his brow. 'Why's that?'

'I haven't fallen into bed with you as soon as you smiled at me.'

'Not yet.' His frown disappeared but something about his slanted smile suggested he thought it was only a matter of time before she did.

Holly put the kitchen table between them, knowing if he so much as touched her she would find it near impossible to resist him. 'So…would you like a cup of tea or something before you go?'

He came around to her side of the kitchen and placed his hands on her hips, his eyes locking on hers. Her heart skipped and her pulse thumped. 'What I'd like is to kiss you again.'

She swallowed and glanced at his mouth, her heart rate going into overdrive. 'I'm not sure that's such a great idea…'

He tipped up her chin so her gaze met his. 'Just a kiss. Nothing else, okay?'

Holly pressed her lips together to try to stop them from tingling in anticipation but if anything it made it worse. Her lips were branded with the texture and feel of his. Who knew a kiss could be so exciting? So enthralling? 'I guess one more kiss would be okay...'

His mouth came down towards her as if in slow motion, every millimetre of the journey ramping up her desire. When he touched down on her lips she gave a soft murmur of approval, her arms winding up around his neck to bring her body closer to the hot hard heat of his. His mouth moved with passionate deliberation, his tongue meeting hers in a sexy tango that made her whole body shiver with longing.

Their first kiss hadn't been a fluke. This one was just as spellbinding, sweeping her up into a vortex of need that coursed through her body like a fast-running tide. His lips were both hard and soft, teasing and tantalising. His tongue flicked against hers in an erotic dance step that triggered a storm of need within her body. She whimpered against the crushing pressure of his mouth, giving herself up to the sensual assault like someone quitting a long-held diet. She feasted on his mouth, relishing in the pressure of it, the allure of his lips and tongue playing with hers.

One of his hands moved from her hips to press into the small of her back, the other sliding up to cradle her face. His mouth clamped to hers with increasing urgency, his body deliciously hard against her. She moved against him, searching for more of that wonderful friction, but he suddenly pulled back and held her apart from him, his breathing heavy and uneven.

He gave another crooked smile. 'I'd better stop before I can't stop.'

Holly knew she should be feeling relieved he had called a halt, but instead she felt disappointed. Achingly disappointed. Her body was on fire and never had she wanted a man more than this one. She looked into his dark blue eyes and wondered if he could tell how much she wanted him to kiss her again. Not once. Not twice but thousands of times. 'I guess we'd better stop, then.' Was that her voice? That whisper-soft thread of sound? That sound of desperation and tantalised but unsatisfied need?

Zack moved closer again as if drawn by a magnetic force, his thumb brushing over the curve of her lower lip. 'You have the most kissable mouth.'

Holly inched closer to him, unable to resist the lure of his body. She slid her hands up the wall of his chest, delighting in the feel of his hard, toned muscles against her hands. It made her wonder what it would be like to be crushed beneath his weight, pleasured by not just his mouth but by his potent male body.

Her wayward thoughts jarred her out of his embrace. She lowered her hands from his chest and took a step back. Where was her resolve when she needed it? She wasn't going to be seduced by him. He was expecting her to fall into his arms like every other woman he showed an interest in. He had selected her at that party, making her his new target, his new and challenging mission of seduction. She would be falling into the same category as every other lover he'd had if she succumbed to his charm.

But if he was disappointed in her stepping away from him he didn't show it. If anything, his indolent smile seemed to suggest he knew exactly what she was thinking.

'So what's the deal for the engagement party next month? Shall I book somewhere for us to stay overnight?' His eyes did their twinkling thing. 'We'll have to share a room or people will wonder if our relationship is genuine.'

Eek! Why hadn't she thought through the details a little more carefully? Holly thought of her parents, still in love after so many years, who rarely spent a night apart. They believed a couple who slept together stayed together. Her parents would expect her and Zack to stay at their house. Would they accept her excuse for not sharing a room with Zack? What would *be* her excuse? She couldn't bear another lecture from her mother about having a healthy sex life. But nor could she bear her family finding out her engagement was a charade. At least she had a few weeks to come up with some sort of excuse.

'I'll get back to you on that... We've got a month

to make arrangements…' Why did she have to sound so vague? As if she was hedging her bets?

'I'd be happy to share if you're up for it.'

Up for it? That was the whole damn problem. Holly was *too* up for it. She was so up for it her body was pulsing with desire. It was all she could think about. Sharing a bed with him. Sharing her body with him. Holly kept her posture stiff and determined even though her resolve to resist him was sagging like a wilted daisy. 'You're not my type. And I'm pretty certain I'm not yours.'

His eyes darkened to midnight blue. 'You felt like my type when I kissed you.' He moved closer and brushed her lower lip with the pad of his thumb, sending her senses spinning like skates on slippery ice. 'Don't you want to explore the chemistry we've got going, hmm?'

'What chemistry?' Holly affected a disinterested tone.

His hand slid under the weight of her hair and he brought his mouth down to just above hers, his warm breath teasing her lips. 'This chemistry.'

CHAPTER FOUR

ZACK HAD NEVER kissed a more gorgeous-tasting mouth. The taste, the texture, the temptation just about blew the top of his head off. Her lips were pillow soft and moved against his with such fervour he had trouble controlling himself. He couldn't stop himself from going back for more. And more. And more. How the hell had he thought he could stop at one kiss? Her mouth was the most responsive mouth he'd ever kissed. It felt like he'd been kissing her for years. Not in a boring, been-there-done-that-hundreds-of-times way, but with a relaxed familiarity that made him realise how deeply in tune his body was with hers. The first time his lips had met hers something had clicked. It was like suddenly recalling the steps to a dance you'd thought you'd long forgotten.

The softness of Holly's mouth had surprised him from the first time he'd kissed her. The softness and the sweetness—sweetness he craved like a potent drug. She tasted of vanilla and cinnamon with a hint of strawberry from her lip gloss—most of which he'd kissed away. He would never be able to look at a strawberry again without thinking about her. Her tongue danced with his in a sexy tango that made his groin swell and throb with need. He could feel the building pressure in his pelvis, the tight ache of his flesh against her softer, deliciously feminine frame.

He couldn't remember a time when a kiss had got him so worked up. It was like his hormones had gone crazy, sending pulses of lust firing through his flesh in sharp shooting darts and piercing arrows. His body was tingling from head to foot where it was in contact with hers and he ached to feel her against him, skin on skin.

He pressed her back against the nearest wall, devouring her mouth, breathing in the fresh flowery scent of her, his senses going wild with longing. Everything about her delighted him: her body, her brain and her bold determination to resist the chemistry that sizzled between them. She was making him work as he'd never worked before. Seduction was a game he played—and played well. He knew when a woman was interested, and consent to him was a priority. Always. He wasn't an egotistical jerk who thought *no* meant *yes*. He respected a woman's right to say no at any stage of making love. And it thrilled him to feel her response to him. Thrilled and excited him because he knew it wouldn't be long before she gave herself to him.

Holly's mouth moved with sweet urgency beneath his, her arms going around his neck, her fingers playing with his hair making shivers shoot up and down his spine. He put a hand to the small of her back and brought her against the throbbing ache of his body. She gave a soft whimper and her teeth grazed his lower lip in a kittenish bite that made his skin tingle all over. Her tongue met his and darted and dived around it in a flickering dance that had erotic overtones. He wanted to surge into her wet warmth and take them both to heaven.

Wanted. Wanted. Wanted.

It was a chant pounding in his blood. A primal thrumming beat so strong, so powerful he could feel it in every pore of his flesh. He had never felt such overwhelming desire for a woman.

What was it about Holly that stirred his senses into such frenzy?

He planted his hand on the wall behind her head and lifted his mouth off the tantalising temptation of hers. 'See what I mean about chemistry?'

'Erm…yes…' Her cheeks were a faint shade of pink, her mouth cherry red from his kisses and her creamy chin grazed from his stubble. Seeing that mark on her skin made something in his chest slip, like his heart had shifted from its moorings.

Zack touched her chin with his finger. 'I've given you beard rash. Sorry.' His voice came out as scratchy as his stubble.

Her toffee-brown eyes were luminous, her tongue sneaking out to lick her lips, and desire hit him like a punch. She put her finger to her chin, tracing over the same spot his finger had moments earlier. 'That's okay…' Her voice was so soft and breathless he had to strain his ears to hear it.

Zack leaned down to press a light-as-air kiss to her mouth but when he pulled away her lips clung to his like silk did to something rough. He traced her mouth with a lazy finger, watching as she swayed towards him, her eyelashes going down to half-mast.

Yep. You've got this.

But then she suddenly blinked and straightened and pressed her lips together as if she'd read his mind. 'If you change your mind about the party next month…'

He took one of her hands and brought it up to his mouth, planting a kiss to her bent knuckles. 'I won't change my mind.'

She pulled her hand out of his hold and dipped out from under his arm, turning to give him a tremulous smile. 'I'll see you in four weeks, then. Shall we say around noon on the Saturday?'

Why was she pulling away from him when it was clear she wanted him as much as he wanted her? Zack wasn't going to let her get away with putting a whole month of distance between them. His body was already feeling the pain of separation. He could barely cope with four minutes without seeing her let alone four weeks. 'I want to see you before then.'

Her chin came up a fraction, her eyes bright with a spark of defiance. 'I'm afraid that's not possible. I'm busy until then.'

He locked his gaze with hers. 'We're engaged. It's expected that we'll spend every available moment outside work together. And we need to get you a ring.'

Her teeth sank into the softness of her bottom lip, her gaze slipping away from his to look at his mouth. She released her lip and brought her gaze back to his, the defiance taken over by a flicker of uncertainty. 'Is a ring really necessary?'

He picked up her left hand and stroked his finger between her knuckles on her ring finger. 'Did your other fiancés buy you rings?'

A shadow moved through her gaze. 'Yes, but that's entirely different because I was engaged to them for real.'

Zack wondered who those men were and why they had left her in the lurch. Jilting a bride was a low act, in his opinion. If a relationship wasn't working, then why not say so in private instead of ditching someone in such a public and humiliating way? He kept hold of her hand, absently stroking the back of it with his thumb. 'Were you in love with either of them?'

Her teeth began to savage her lip again. 'I thought so at the time...'

'And now?'

Her eyes met his briefly, only to dip to his mouth once more. She let out a long sigh and stepped out of his hold, running a hand through the mane of her hair in a distracted manner. The movement of her hair released the scent of flowers and he longed to bury his head in its fragrant strands.

'No...' she said. 'I was feeling the pressure of being the firstborn daughter to happily married parents who think the only way a girl can be happy is to have a husband by her side.' She hugged her arms around her body and glanced at him again. 'The first man who showed an interest in me and I fancied I was in love with him. I can see now how much pressure I put on him. There were signs we weren't all that well suited, but did I take notice of them? No. I was too caught up in wedding fever. So much so that I was the one who proposed to him.' A tide of colour swept into her face and she turned her head away, as if shamed by her revelation.

'So what happened the next time?'

Holly let out a humourless laugh. 'I met Peter eighteen months after Owen called off the wedding. He seemed keen on the idea of marrying but, in hindsight, I think that was more because I didn't want to sleep with him until he made a solid commitment.' She screwed up her mouth. 'At least this time he was the one who proposed to me, but it was hardly what you would call romantic.'

'How did he propose?'

'He said, and I quote, "How about we get hitched?"'
Holly rolled her eyes. 'More fool me for accepting
such a lousy proposal. He was having it off with his
personal trainer the whole time we were together. He
told me she was his second cousin twice removed.'

Zack frowned. 'That's really low. I know I have a
reputation as a playboy, but the one thing I've never
done is cheat on a partner, no matter how casual the
relationship.'

Holly gave him a twisted lip movement that
wasn't quite a smile. 'Have you ever been in love?'

'No.'

Her nutmeg-brown eyes held his for a beat or two.
'That sounded a rather emphatic response.'

Zack shrugged. 'That's because it's true. I've
never felt that way about anyone.'

'Not even a tiny flutter of your closed-off heart?'
There was a pert note to her voice that made him wonder if she knew how attracted he was to her—far more
attracted than he had ever been to anyone before.

Zack affected a casual smile even though his
heart was doing a damn fine impression of doing
some serious fluttering right then and there. It felt
like someone had opened an aviary inside his chest.
'Nope.'

Her smile was tight and fleeting and she glanced
towards the door. 'I should let you get on with your
evening. Thanks again for the flowers.'

'Have dinner with me.'

Her chin came back up. 'Do you always command people to do as you wish?'

Zack was getting off on her starchy tone. She was so damn cute he could barely stand it. 'You have to eat, don't you? We might as well do it together. We're engaged, remember?'

Her mouth pursed and it made him want to kiss it back into shape. 'Stop reminding me.'

'I'll give you five minutes to get ready,' Zack said and took out his phone. 'Well, will you look at that. That Tweet about us has gone viral. I'd better give my dad a call before—' His phone began to ring and he saw his father's name come up on the screen. He mouthed, 'Excuse me,' to Holly and turned to answer the call. 'Dad, are you okay?'

'I was going to ask you the same question,' his father said. 'What's going on? Someone told me they heard you just got engaged. Why didn't you tell me the other night?'

Zack was conscious of Holly hovering close by. 'Yeah, well, I hadn't asked her then,' he said, winking at her. 'I didn't think she'd say yes, but she did.'

'I'm thrilled for you!' His dad's voice was as upbeat as a motivational speaker. 'My boy's getting married. At long last.'

'I got tired of being single,' Zack said, mentally crossing his fingers at all the white lies he was telling. 'I'm ready to settle down.' He was acting like a man who had fallen in love for the first time. He would never be that man, but it didn't mean he couldn't act like it. Ruthless of him? You bet. Maybe he should have pursued an acting career. Who knew he had such a gift?

'When do I get to meet her?' his dad asked.

Zack glanced at Holly, who was blushing like a hothouse rose. 'I'll give you a call soon to arrange dinner with us. Sorry you had to find out via someone else. I should've given you a heads-up the other night.'

'It's okay, son. As long as you're happy, that's all I care about.'

Zack ended the call and looked at Holly. 'As you probably heard—my dad sends his congratulations.'

She pulled at her lip with her teeth, her cheeks still stained pink. 'I'm sorry I didn't believe you about being at the theatre with him the other night. I assumed you were with someone else. A female someone else.'

'It's okay. I would've much preferred to be with you, but my dad needs a bit of support now and again.' Zack knew he had stepped over a line by revealing more about his relationship with his father than he normally would, but for some reason he didn't feel as uncomfortable about it as he'd expected.

Concern shone in her gaze. 'Is he unwell?'

Zack pocketed his phone. 'He broke up with a

partner a few months ago. He's finding it a little hard to move on.'

'How long were they together?'

He gave a rueful twist of his mouth. 'Long enough for my father to make comparisons between her and my mother, who he still holds up as the ideal model of a wife even though she divorced him twenty-four years ago.'

'That must have been tough on you,' Holly said, screwing up her forehead in a frown. 'What were you? Ten?'

'Yep. Ten going on thirty. It was tough mostly because my dad fell apart.' Zack was surprised by how easy it was to talk to her about his past. 'I'm an only child so it fell to me to pick up the pieces.' He released a sigh of frustration. Twenty-four years of frustration. 'It still falls on me. He can't seem to move on. Every time he suffers another break-up it brings back all the unresolved issues he had with my mother.'

'I'm sorry for misjudging you the other night.' Holly's tone was softened with remorse. 'You sound like a good son. He's lucky to have you to support him.'

'I do my best, but it's tough at times. That's why I decided to run with our engagement after Kendra sent that Tweet. My dad's been blaming himself for my playboy lifestyle. I figured if I showed him I was in a committed relationship it might take some of that guilt off him.' Zack stretched his mouth into a rueful smile. 'I don't normally talk about this stuff to anyone. You're a good listener.'

She smiled back. 'I could say the same about you.'

He couldn't drag his eyes away from the sweet curve of her lips. He moved closer and slid his hand along the side of her face, lifting her chin to mesh her gaze with his. 'If we don't go and get some dinner soon, I might change my mind and eat you instead.'

She gave a delicate shiver as if his erotic promise had secretly thrilled her. She slipped out of his hold, her colour high. 'I'll go and get changed. Please…make yourself at home.' She stepped back and bumped into the kitchen table. 'Oops. Silly me.' She gave him a flustered smile and turned and disappeared out of the room.

Holly took a deep steadying breath when she got to her bedroom. Her heart was thumping like it had been given a shot of adrenaline and her body was tingling from the sensual threat Zack had promised. She glanced at her reflection in the mirror and saw the patch of beard rash on her chin and something in her stomach turned over. Why did she have no willpower around him? His kisses were like a drug she couldn't get enough of and his touch made her senses turn cartwheels. She felt annoyed with herself for being so cynical about his 'date' the other night. He clearly had a good relationship with his father—a loving and supportive one that made her admire him all the more.

She'd been right about one thing, though. His parents' divorce had made an impact on him. A big impact. His reluctance to commit fully to a relationship made perfect sense when she thought about his father's struggles that Zack had witnessed first-hand.

Holly turned away from the mirror and opened her wardrobe. What was she going to wear? She had always been too busy working to pay much attention to fashion. She wore casual clothes to work because floristry could be messy at times. She had a couple of nice outfits that got her by, but nothing in the same class as some of his glamorous lovers. How would she measure up in her boring off-the-peg little black dress?

She sighed and stripped off her work gear and stepped into her dress, smoothing it over her stomach and thighs. She brushed her hair and then scooped it up on top of her head in a casual knot, leaving some tendrils hanging down around her face. She scrabbled around on her dressing table for a set of pearl droplet earrings her parents had given her for her last birthday and put them on. She freshened up her make-up and sprayed her wrists with perfume. She slipped on a pair of heels and grabbed a cashmere pashmina— another birthday present, this time from her sister Katie—and wrapped it around her shoulders.

She tilted her head from side to side, wondering

why Zack had chosen her as his latest seduction target. She wasn't a beauty, not in the traditional sense of the word. Her three sisters were the beauties in the family. She was kind of okay but in a forgettable girl-next-door way.

Holly blew out a sigh and picked up her evening purse. Her man drought was over but pretending to be engaged to Zack Knight was surely the craziest thing she'd ever done.

And by far the most exciting.

Holly came back out to the sitting room, where Zack was waiting for her. He was scrolling through the messages or emails on his phone…or maybe he was reading his Twitter feed. He stood when she came into the room, his gaze travelling over her figure with blatant male appraisal. 'Wow. You look amazing.'

She could feel her cheeks glowing and wondered if she would ever get tired of hearing him compliment her. No. Never. He made her feel more feminine, more attractive, more desirable than she'd ever felt before. Why was she insisting on resisting him? No man had ever made her feel so attractive. No man had ever touched her and made her burn with need. When he looked at her with those dark blue smouldering-with-lust eyes, her insides quaked with longing—a longing so intense it threatened to overrule every one of her reasons for not getting involved with him. 'Thank you,' she said with a smile.

'I called a mate of mine who owns a jewellery shop,' he said. 'I've done two of his divorces so far and counting. He designs his own exclusive range. We can go to his studio before dinner—he's staying open specially for us.'

Holly blinked and her smile fell away. 'A jewellery designer sounds hideously expensive. Why can't we just use one from a chain store?'

'This engagement of ours might not be the real deal but I insist any jewellery you wear from me will be,' Zack said. 'I'm not having people think I'm too tight to buy my fiancée a decent rock.'

Holly drew her pashmina closer around her shoulders. 'I'll accept a ring, but only on the proviso that I give it back to you once we end our engagement. Agreed?'

'No.' His tone was as firm as a punctuation mark. 'You will keep it. I insist. Think of it as a gift.'

Her chin came up. 'I don't accept expensive gifts from men.'

'Even ones you're in love with?'

Holly affected a laugh. 'I'm not in love with you.'

He gave a slow smile and stroked a lazy finger down the slope of her burning cheek. 'This is probably a good time to set some ground rules.' His finger moved to the patch of stubble rash on her chin, passing over it in a faint movement that made her skin tingle. 'No falling in love, okay? This isn't for ever.'

Holly pulled away from him before she went into

a mesmerised trance. 'Are you saying that for your benefit or mine? What if you fall in love with me? Have you thought about *that* possibility?'

Something flickered through his gaze but his smile never faltered. 'There's no way of saying this without it sounding like an insult, but no, I'm not going to fall in love with you or anybody.'

Holly wasn't sure why she should be feeling such a painful stab of disappointment. She didn't want him to fall in love with her. Why would she? She didn't want to fall in love with anyone ever again. Having a fling with him was something she was prepared to consider. More than prepared. But falling in love with him? Not going to happen. 'Maybe you haven't met the right woman. The one who holds the key to your cynical heart.'

He jangled his car keys in his pocket, his expression now as inscrutable as a blank canvas. 'We should get going. Nathan will be waiting for us.'

Holly went with Zack to where his car was parked out on the street. It was a top-model sports car, a deep navy blue, the same colour as his eyes. He helped her into the passenger seat and she thought back to all the times her exes had left her to fend for herself. She might be a feminist, but she still loved it when a man held a door open for her. She breathed in his aftershave as she moved past him to get in the car, her senses so finely tuned to him she was aware of every point of contact. The slightest brush of his fingers was enough to make her heart skip a beat. When their gazes met, her stomach slipped like a foot missing a rung on a ladder.

When he got behind the wheel she was conscious of how close he was to her, his strong muscular thighs within touching distance, his hand on the gear lever close enough for her to see the dark hairs sprinkled over the back of his hand. She sucked in a breath and pulled her seat belt down, clipping it in place, wishing she could restrain her body's traitorous longings just as easily. Did he know the battle she was fighting? The battle to resist his lethal charm. The battle she was fast losing because her body was a traitor. It was drawn to him like the ocean was drawn towards the shore. An unstoppable tide of longing that rolled through her in slow, rhythmic waves, washing away her willpower like shallow footprints in sand.

Zack started the car with a throaty roar that sent a shudder through her body. *Sheesh*. Even his car made her think of sex.

He glanced at her with a smile. 'Ready?'

'Ready.' Holly wasn't sure if she was or not. Accepting an engagement ring from a man who didn't love her was becoming a pattern for her, it seemed. But she had to get her business back on track and she had to get through her sister's engagement party next month. She couldn't allow any misgivings about her 'engagement' with Zack to distract her from her mission. She didn't want to think too much about how long they would continue the charade. He'd mentioned weeks, possibly months, but she knew from the gossip pages he never stayed with a lover longer than a month, sometimes less. She'd found it kind of sweet how he wanted to convince his father he was a reformed playboy, but how long before Zack got restless and wanted to move on?

It would be foolish of her to think he might not want to end the charade, that he might fall in love with her and…

Holly skirted away from the thought like someone avoiding a muddy puddle. She was over the fairy tale. Over. Over. Over. The fairy tale happened to other people, not to her. Every time she'd bought into the fairy tale it had handed her a poisoned apple. Two poisoned apples. Her involvement with Zack wasn't a poisoned apple—it was forbidden fruit and she was going to enjoy every deliciously tempting bite.

'Tell me about your family.' Zack's deep, mellifluous voice broke through her reverie.

'Both my parents are high school teachers,' Holly said. 'They fell in love the first time they met in the school staffroom on the first day of term. I have three sisters. All of them are younger than me. Two of them are married and the youngest, Belinda, is the one who just got engaged.'

'No pressure or anything.'

Holly grimaced. 'Tell me about it. They can't seem to accept I want to remain single.'

He sent her a sideways glance. 'So you're not after the fairy tale? The big church white wedding with all the trimmings?'

Holly gave a shudder. 'No way. I'm done with the fairy tale.' She turned in her seat to look at him. 'What about your family? What sort of work do your parents do?'

A muscle tensed in his jaw and his hands on the steering wheel tightened a fraction. 'My father is a civil servant. He mostly works part-time these days.'

'And your mother?'

His mouth came up at one side in a cynical slant. 'She does lunch. Her husband—one of three she's had since my father—is a wealthy property developer. She hasn't worked since she married my dad when she got pregnant with me.'

Holly wondered if his reasons for being a divorce lawyer had something to do with his background. Divorce was always hard on kids; even the most amicable of divorces could leave a mark on children. 'Who did you spend most of your time with growing up?'

'My father.' He opened and closed his hands on the steering wheel as if he was conscious of gripping it too tightly. 'My mother didn't want custody.'

Holly bit her lip, thinking of the love her mother had for her and her sisters. She couldn't imagine a single circumstance where her mother would have relinquished custody in the event of a divorce. Didn't most parents share custodial arrangements? Or at least want to? 'That must have been awfully tough on you, especially as a ten-year-old.'

He gave an indifferent shrug but she noticed his hands hadn't totally relaxed their grip on the steering wheel. 'I survived.'

'Did you see much of her during your childhood? I mean, even though she didn't want custody?'

'Occasionally. Birthdays, that sort of thing.'

'Is your parents' divorce the reason why you became a divorce lawyer?'

'I guess to some degree, yes.' He glanced over his shoulder before he deftly switched lanes. 'My father was completely blindsided by my mother's demand for a divorce. He'd worked hard at keeping them together. Too hard, in my opinion. He's much better off without her, but unfortunately he doesn't believe that.'

Holly frowned. 'But you said they divorced when you were ten. Isn't that a little too long to be hoping someone will come back to you?'

He gave a frustrated-sounding sigh. 'Try telling my father that. He believes my mother is the only woman he will ever truly love. That's why his subsequent relationships always fail. His new partners never measure up.'

'Do you see much of your mother now?'

His mouth twisted. 'I'm a dutiful son.'

'But not a devoted one?'

'No.'

His one-word answer seemed to contain a host of intriguing backstory Holly longed to explore. His childhood had been so different from hers. She had never once doubted her parents' love for her and or their love for each other. It had given her childhood a warm cosy blanket of security that to this day she still relied on. She couldn't imagine how devastating it would have been for Zack to have his mother walk out on him and his father when he was only ten years old. To watch his father crumble emotionally and feel so powerless as a child to do anything to help him. And then to only see his mother occasionally while he was growing up. What had that done to him emotionally? Had it made him bitter and distrustful about long-term relationships? Was he commitment-shy in case the woman he loved walked out on him like his mother had done to him and his father?

'I guess watching your dad go through such heartache for so long must make you pretty wary about relationships,' Holly said. 'And the divorce work you do must reinforce that wariness.'

'I keep my relationships pretty simple.'

'And short.'

He glanced at her with a wry smile. 'So you do read the gossip pages.'

Holly could feel her cheeks heating. 'At the hairdresser's. It's hard to find a magazine these days without a picture of you in it with your latest squeeze. Do you have a penchant for blondes?'

His eyes glinted. 'Redheads are my current thing.'

Holly gave him a mock glare. 'My hair isn't red. It's chestnut.'

'It's beautiful, like burnished copper. It's the first thing I noticed about you. That and your gorgeous figure.' He sent her a wicked grin. 'Oh, and your mouth.'

Holly could feel herself glowing from his compliments. She had always been self-conscious about her wild hair and curvy figure. But when his gaze ran over her with such molten heat she felt like the most beautiful and sexy woman on the planet.

The jewellery design studio was situated in central London. Holly had heard of the designer Nathan Strickland, who made bespoke jewellery for the well-heeled and wealthy. Never in her wildest dreams had she imagined she would be one day sitting in his studio being shown a tray of exquisite engagement rings.

'Do you have a particular design in mind?' Nathan asked once introductions were over.

Holly was still recovering from the shock of realising there weren't any price tags in sight. That could only mean one thing—no way could she have ever afforded any item on show. Not even a pair of earrings. Not even one earring. 'Erm...I like simple designs.' She pointed to the smallest setting she could find in the tray. The solitaire diamond was set in a classic design and winked at her as if to say, *Pick me!*

'You like this one?' Zack said, lifting it out and turning it to the light.

'Yes, it's lovely...'

'Your fiancée has excellent taste,' Nathan said to Zack. 'But then, why wouldn't she since she's chosen you, hey?'

Zack grinned, took Holly's hand and slipped the ring on her finger. 'Well, look at that. A perfect fit. It must be an omen.'

Holly looked at the ring on her finger and suppressed a shiver at the way Zack's tanned hand contrasted with her lighter, creamy-toned skin. She couldn't stop imagining his hands on other parts of her body. On her breasts, on her belly. Between her legs... 'It's a beautiful ring...' She looked up at Zack, her stomach slipping when his eyes meshed with hers. 'But are you sure?'

He gave her hand a gentle squeeze. 'Never surer.'

Holly knew he was acting for the benefit of his friend watching on, but it didn't stop a secret part of her wondering what it would be like to choose a ring with a man who truly loved her and wanted to spend the rest of his life with her. Did such a man exist for her? Neither of her ex-fiancés had consulted her on her choice of ring but had presented her with ones she hadn't really liked.

How strange that her fake fiancé would be prepared to buy her such a gorgeous ring and not blink an eye at the expense.

They said their goodbyes to Nathan and left the studio to head to the restaurant Zack had booked for dinner. It was a short walking distance from the studio and Zack took her arm and looped it through one of his. 'Stop frowning, Holly,' he said, glancing down at her while they waited for a pedestrian signal. 'It wasn't that expensive.'

'I can't believe you were prepared to pay that much for a ring for a woman you're not in love with,' Holly said.

'I told you why. I don't want people thinking you're not worth a decent ring.'

Holly couldn't help feeling a little thrilled he'd insisted on buying such a lovely ring for her. She kept glancing at it on her finger, marvelling at the way it suited her hand so well. But then, walking side by side with his arm around her, she felt the same strange sense of rightness, as if they had been walking arm in arm for years. 'My exes bought me rings I hated, and Peter, my second fiancé, bought me a fake diamond. I didn't realise it was fake until after we broke up. But, given how things panned out, I should've guessed earlier.'

'The more I hear about your exes the more I want to knock their heads together,' Zack said, frowning.

'Yes, well, the thing is, Peter bought his new wife the real thing,' Holly said. 'She came into the shop soon after they announced their engagement and brandished it under my nose. And she made sure I could see she was pregnant when she came in recently. She's having twins this summer.'

He slipped his arm around her waist and drew her closer. 'I'm sorry you've had such jerks mess you around. I can see why you've been so reluctant to put yourself out there again.'

But she had put herself out there again, hadn't she? She was walking arm in arm with the hottest guy in London and she was wearing his gorgeous ring. Holly knew if she wasn't careful she could be in real danger of not just bruising her heart this time but having it break into a thousand confetti-like pieces.

CHAPTER FIVE

A SHORT TIME LATER, Zack sat opposite Holly at a table in the restaurant he'd chosen. He couldn't stop his gaze from drifting to her slender hand where his 'engagement' ring was winking at him. Sure, it was a lot of money for a ring that wasn't going to be used in the real sense, but he was adamant Holly wouldn't feel used or cheapened in any way by their temporary relationship. Their engagement charade was supposed to be a win-win and he didn't want her to feel exploited in any way.

But it was kind of weird how right it had felt to slip that ring on her finger. Not just how nice it looked on her hand and how it was a perfect fit, but how...*right* it felt. He couldn't imagine ever putting a ring on anyone else's hand. Before now he'd never wanted to. But the ring wasn't staying on her hand any longer than a few weeks, tops. He was happy to play the role of Mr Right Now but Mr Right For Ever...?

Forget about it.

Holly glanced at her ring and her teeth began to chew at her lower lip. Zack placed his hand on top of hers. 'Hey. Enough about the ring, okay?' he said, softening it with a smile. 'It's the only one I'm ever going to buy someone, so indulge me.'

She was still frowning. 'But what if you were to fall in love one day? You might change your mind about marrying and having a family.'

Zack withdrew his hand and picked up his wine glass instead. The thought of falling in love privately terrified him. He wasn't emotionally cold by any means. He felt—and felt deeply—but he was careful, guarded with how he handled romantic relationships. Wary of allowing himself to get so attached to someone he couldn't imagine life without them. He'd seen too much with his dad. Destroyed by his love for a woman who wasn't capable of loving him back. He too had felt the pain of being abandoned by the one person who should have loved him more than life itself. But his mother had left—and left gladly. Never coming back for him. He had stood at the window every time a car came down the driveway, hoping, praying it was his mother coming back.

But his hopes and prayers had been in vain. It had made him distrustful of love. It seemed to him to be an unreliable emotion, a fickle feeling that could change in a blink.

No. His heart was fine the way it was. Protected. Secure. Safe.

'What about you?' Zack asked. 'Don't all young women want to fall in love and get married and have babies one day?'

Holly let out a blustery sigh. 'I used to want that more than anything but I can't bear the thought of being publicly humiliated again.'

'You might be luckier the next time around.'

Her smile wasn't quite a smile. 'Nope. I told you before—I'm done with the fairy tale. And as for kids—I'll settle with being a devoted aunty to my future nephews and nieces.'

Zack had met plenty of commitment cynics in his time, but Holly's cynicism seemed rather sad to him. Tragic even. It was far easier for him to build a satisfying life without the ties of a family. But he thought most women longed for a family, didn't they? He could imagine her surrounded by a brood of rosy-cheeked children, showering them with the warm nurturing affection he had missed out on as a child. 'You might change your mind one day.'

Her eyes met his in a pert challenge. 'So might you.'

He laughed but even to his ears it sounded a little forced. No way was he going to end up like his dad, left holding the baby. Or a ten-year-old kid. He often wondered if that was why his father had struggled so much to cope, because he hadn't expected to parent a child on his own. 'I've spent my entire adult life making sure I don't get anyone pregnant. I can't see that changing any time soon, if ever.'

'You don't like kids?'

'I love kids. It's what happens to them when parents get divorced that worries me.'

'You might not get divorced,' she said, picking up her wine glass. 'You might be one of the lucky ones.'

'Everyone thinks they'll be one of the lucky ones when they first start out,' Zack said. 'But a successful relationship is not up to one person—it's up to two. I saw that with my parents. Dad was doing all he could to be a supportive and loving husband and it still wasn't enough. My mother found someone more interesting.'

'She had an affair?'

'One of several,' Zack said. 'It devastated my dad. He forgave her the first couple of times she strayed, but then she ran off with the local vicar in the village. It created an enormous scandal people still talk about to this day.' It felt strange to be talking so openly about something still so painful to even think about, much less talk about with someone he'd only met a week ago. But somehow with Holly it was different. It felt natural to be telling her about his past.

Natural and safe.

'I can't imagine how difficult and painful that must have been for you as a young boy,' Holly said. 'And for your dad. I've been lucky with my parents.

They're still in love with each other after thirty-three years of marriage.'

'Good to know the fairy tale still happens occasionally.'

Holly's expression looked wistful. 'Yes...'

He raised his glass in a toast. 'To us. The non-fairy-tale pursuers.'

She clinked her glass against his. 'To the non-fairy-tale pursuers.'

It was late by the time Zack drove Holly back to her flat that evening. She hadn't wanted the evening to end. The food had been delicious but it was his company that had made the evening so enjoyable. He was funny and charming but when he'd shared some of the pain of his lonely childhood she'd realised behind his laugh-a-minute manner he was a deeply sensitive and caring man. Perhaps, at times, even a lonely man. The way he worried about his father, even pretending to be engaged in order to make his dad feel less guilty, demonstrated that. She felt more and more annoyed at herself for not believing him the other night at the theatre. She had allowed her jaundiced view of men to blind her to the truth.

Holly unlocked the door of her flat and turned to face Zack. 'Would you like to come in for a nightcap?'

His eyes dipped to her mouth, a flicker of something passing over his features. 'I'm not sure that's a good idea tonight.'

Why? A stab of disappointment pierced Holly's self-esteem. She was so certain he was going to ask to come in and kiss her. Maybe even do *more* than kiss her. Had she somehow misread the crackling chemistry between them? Made more of their evening than he had? It was a little terrifying to realise how much she wanted him to come in. How much she wanted him to press her back against the nearest wall and kiss her senseless. 'Okay. Maybe some other time…' She tried to keep her voice light and carefree but even she could hear the jangling chord of uncertainty.

'Holly.' His deep and rough tone brought her gaze back up to his. His eyes were as dark as a midnight sky with glints of lust sprinkled like stars. 'You know what will happen if I come inside.'

Holly licked her lips and tried to slow her suddenly racing pulse. 'I would make coffee or fix you a port or…or something.'

His lifted his hand to her face and brushed the backs of his bent knuckles against her heated cheek. Every pore of her skin shuddered, his touch causing an earthquake beneath her epidermis. 'It's the "or something" that's keeping me on this side of the door.'

Holly wasn't sure if they were talking about nightcaps or something else. But why shouldn't it be about something else? The something else she wanted like she had never wanted before. She could feel it building in her body even now. The pulse of longing thrumming in her blood, the low deep ache in her core that intensified whenever he looked at her with his simmering I-want-you gaze.

But begging him to make love to her was not something she was comfortable doing. He was used to women elbowing each other out of the way to get to him. She was not going to do the same. If he was having second thoughts about getting too close to her, then so be it. He wasn't the only one who had self-control, not to mention self-respect. Holly gave a disingenuous laugh and pointed her finger between herself and him. 'Oh, I get it. You thought I wanted you to come in and *sleep* with me? Sorry, but I'm not that kind of girl.' *Or I wasn't until I met you.*

His mouth tilted in a smile so knowing she might as well have been standing there naked with a sign on her saying, Take Me, I'm Yours. 'I'll give you a call in a couple of days. *Ciao.*'

Holly listened to the sound of his footsteps as he left and pushed down her disappointment like someone trying to stuff a pillow into a matchbox. Damn him for making her want him so much. Damn him for having such sensual power over her. Damn him for being the most irresistible man she had ever met. She would have to be careful how she handled him in future. She couldn't allow him to mess with her head.

Or worse—her heart.

* * *

A couple of days later, Zack leaned back in his office chair and fiddled with his pen, his gaze wandering to the view outside. The intermittent rain and occasional bursts of watery sunlight were a reminder of how much he was looking forward to a week in Paris for a law conference next week. In the past, he would have seen a conference as an opportunity to hook up with someone for a casual no-strings fling.

But now he *only* wanted Holly.

What if he asked her to go with him to Paris? If she said yes, it would be another way to assure his dad that his playboy days were behind him. He smiled in anticipation. Another win-win.

She filled his every waking thought and a large proportion of his sleeping ones too. He dreamed of her lying in the bed next to him. Last night he had even reached for her and the jolt of disappointment when he'd found his bed empty had stunned him into a long period of wakefulness. He couldn't remember a time when a woman had had such a potent effect on him. He was like a teenage boy experiencing his first infatuation.

He knew they could have slept together the other night but he wanted to take his time. He was enjoying the flirtation too much. He didn't want his relationship with her to be like all his other relationships. He wasn't exactly sure why... Or was it because it wasn't just his father he wanted to convince he was more than a date-them-and-dump-them playboy?

Zack picked up his phone and dialled Holly's number.

She answered on the seventh ring. 'Hi, Zack.'

'Missed me?'

'Not a bit.'

He gave a low and deep chuckle at the haughtiness of her tone. 'I want to see you tonight.'

'I might not be free.'

He swivelled back and forth on his chair, enjoying the sound of her voice. Enjoying the tussle between her strong will and his. Enjoying the challenge of winning her over, as he knew he eventually would. 'I'll pick you up at seven.'

'Do you live in a big house?'

'Yes, why?'

'I suppose you need all that extra space to house your overblown ego.'

Zack smiled to himself. She was so darn cute when she spoke in that schoolmistress tone. 'You should check it out sometime.'

'Your house or your ego?'

He leaned forward to rest his elbows on his desk, the phone still cradled against his ear. 'Since we're engaged, people will wonder why you're not living with me.'

He heard the swift intake of her breath as if his statement had shocked her. 'I'm not moving in with you, so you can get that idea out of your head right this second.'

'It wasn't an invitation. Simply an observation.'

There was a small silence.

'Don't you have work to do or something?' Holly said.

Zack glanced at the tower of paperwork on his desk. 'Yep. But I'm looking forward to playing later.'

Holly was standing at the window when Zack pulled up in front of her flat later that day. She'd been in two minds about whether to go out with him. The more time she spent with him, the less self-control she had. Even the sound of his voice was enough to set her hormones racing. Zack looked up at her and smiled and her heart gave a skip. She stepped away from the window, annoyed he'd caught her waiting for him like an overly eager teenager going on her first date. But in a way that was exactly what she felt like. She had never felt this level of excitement with her exes. The heady anticipation of being in Zack's company, the thrill of being so blatantly desired—it was enough to set her pulse soaring.

Holly opened the door to his confident knock, schooling her features into a mask of indifference. 'Good evening.' Her voice sounded like she was auditioning for a role as a head housekeeper on a period drama but how else was she going to keep her hands off him? He looked like he'd stepped down off a billboard advertising an exclusive male aftershave, the planes and contours of his cleanly shaven face making her ache to touch him, to trace every millimetre of his smiling mouth.

Zack stepped over the threshold and closed the door behind him. 'Come here.' His tone was commanding. I-want-to-have-sex-with-you-right-now commanding. His sapphire-blue eyes locked on hers with electrifying heat.

Holly had no idea where her resolve had gone, but she stepped into his arms as if someone was pushing her from behind. There was no way she could resist him, nor did she want to. What would be the point? She wanted him. Wanted him with a persistent ache that pulsed deep inside her body. His arms came around her with steely strength, a gasp escaping her mouth just before his came down and covered hers.

His mouth moved with spine-tingling passion against hers, slowly, methodically, tantalisingly. He teased her lips apart with his lips, taking her lower lip between gentle teeth, tugging and releasing until her legs threatened to give way. He went to her lower lip, subjecting it to the same exquisite torture, his tongue stroking over where his teeth had been in a soothing salve that made something in her belly flip-flop-flap like a blown tyre.

'God, I've been looking forward to doing that for the last forty-eight hours.' His words sent a frisson skating over her flesh.

Holly slipped her arms around his neck, her fingers playing with the ends of his wavy hair that brushed his collar. He groaned against her mouth and deepened the kiss with a gliding thrust of his tongue that made her insides clench with desire. She breathed in the clean male scent of him, the lime and lemon and country leather smell that never failed to stir her senses.

His hands stroked up and down her back, one of them settling at the base of her spine to bring her closer to his hard heat. He was powerfully aroused and it thrilled her to think she had that effect on him. She moved against him in an unspoken plea for him to continue. How had she ever thought she could resist him? Her body was aching for him. Aching and weeping with want. Her legs felt heavy; there was a dragging sensation inside her, an empty hollow ache that wouldn't go away.

He moved his mouth to the sensitive place below her ear and she shivered as his stubble grazed her face. 'I want you so bad.' His voice was a low gruff burr as exciting to her as a caress.

'I want you too.'

His eyes held hers with dark intensity. 'Are you sure about this?'

Holly pulled his head down. 'Stop talking. Kiss me. Touch me. Make love to me.'

Zack brought his mouth back down to hers, his arms gathering her close, making her aware of the heat and throb of his body. His tongue played with hers, teasing it into play with brazenly erotic movements that made her tremble with need.

He moved his mouth to her décolletage, his lips and tongue tracing the scaffold of her collarbone, before he dipped his tongue into the hollow between her clavicle. He moved back to the other side of her neck, caressing her with his lips and tongue until every nerve was doing a happy dance. He skimmed one of his hands over her breasts and even through the barrier of her clothes she felt the sensual magic of his touch.

He put a hand behind her to pull down the zip on her dress, the backs of his knuckles against her bare skin making her shiver. He peeled her out of her dress, letting it slip to the floor at her feet, his eyes devouring her. 'You're so beautiful…' There was an edge of wonder in his voice that made her shyness fall away from her as easily and smoothly as her dress.

She began to work on the buttons of his shirt, and as she undid each one she pressed a kiss to his warm hard flesh. She felt him shudder the lower she got, the ridged muscles of his abdomen contracting under her lips. He shrugged himself out of his shirt and it fell to the floor with a whisper of fabric.

He took her by the hand and led her to her bedroom, turning her in his arms once they got inside next to the bed. He gave the single bed a rueful look. 'The last time I had sex in a single bed I was sixteen.'

Holly grimaced. 'Sorry.'

He smiled and pulled her close, his mouth brushing hers. 'Maybe we should wait until I take you back to my place.'

She gripped him by the waist. 'No. I can't wait. I want you now.'

His eyes glinted. 'Impatient little thing, aren't you?'

Holly moved against the bulge of his erection. 'I could say the same about you.'

He slipped one of her bra straps off her shoulder, exposing part of her breast. He bent his head and moved his lips across the upper curve of her breast, his tongue licking a line of fire across her tender skin. He reached behind her to unclip her bra and it fell to the floor by the bed. His eyes feasted on her body and Holly had never felt more desirable. He brought his mouth back to her breast, his lips and tongue tracing each curve before circling her tight nipple. Sensations shot through her flesh, tingling sensations that travelled from her nipple to her inner core. He drew her nipple into his mouth, sucking on her gently, making her wild with longing. He moved to her other breast, exploring it with his lips and tongue, drawing on her nipple with the same exquisitely gentle suction until she was making mewling sounds of need she couldn't remember ever making before. Had she ever felt this aroused? Had she ever had her breasts treated so tenderly? So worshipfully?

Holly put her hands on his waistband, desperate to get him naked. 'You're wearing too many clothes.' She unclipped his belt and pulled it out of the lugs, glancing up at him from beneath her lashes. 'Seems only fair I get to undress you.'

'Go for it, sweetheart.' His voice had such a sexy timbre to it she felt it vibrating in her core.

She slid his zip down and he stepped out of his trousers, standing before her in a pair of close-fitting black undershorts. Tented undershorts. Magnificently, gloriously tented. She skated a finger down the length of him, a frisson passing over her flesh at the thought of him entering her. Stretching her. Filling her. Pleasuring her.

He pulled his undershorts down and captured her hand and held it against the throb of his arousal. 'You make me so hot I can barely stand it.'

'Likewise.' Holly slid her hand up and down his length, watching as ripples of pleasure played out on his features.

After a moment, he pushed her hand away. 'Enough. My turn to torture you.'

Holly shivered as he pulled her down to the bed. He gave her a smouldering look and peeled her knickers down her thighs like he was taking his time unwrapping a much-longed-for gift. 'So damn beautiful…' He traced the seam of her body with a slow finger.

Holly sucked in a breath as he brought his mouth

to her. 'I'm not very good at this... I can never come so—'

'Relax for me, sweetie.' Zack placed a gentle hand on her abdomen, settling her like one did a nervous pet.

Holly had to remind herself to breathe when he lowered his head once more to her body. His breath was a warm caress and then his fingers touched her, sending her senses into overdrive. His lips were next, separating her folds, his tongue moving over her delicate flesh until she was gasping. A tiny ripple turned into a torrent, sensations rushing through her body in ever-increasing waves. Waves that threatened to overpower her consciousness. And then bliss...a floaty feeling of sublime pleasure coursing through every inch of her flesh.

Zack propped himself up on one elbow beside her. 'Knew you could do it.'

Holly suddenly felt shy that he had witnessed her at her most vulnerable. She had never orgasmed during oral sex before. She had always pretended to get it over with because the sheer intimacy of it had threatened her. Frightened her. But with Zack it had felt so...so *right*. She watched the pathway of her finger tracing his collarbone rather than meet his gaze. 'You've probably done that hundreds, no thousands of times.'

He brought her chin up with his finger, his gaze dark and lustrous. 'I don't do it with everyone.'

She tried not to read too much into his comment but her heart lifted all the same. Did he see her as somehow special? Different from his other lovers? 'Would you like me to do the same to you?'

'Not just now.' He brushed her lips with his mouth. 'I want to make love to you. But first I have to get a condom.' He got off the bed and walked over to where he'd left his trousers on the floor. He came back in carrying the tiny foil packet and she marvelled at how gorgeous he looked naked. Strong and fit and lightly tanned, his abdomen rippling with toned muscles.

Holly made room for him on the bed, not an easy task as there wasn't much to spare. He came down beside her and gathered her close, his mouth coming down to hers in a lingering kiss. He moved his mouth down to her breasts, caressing them with his lips and tongue, ramping up her need for him until she was writhing and whimpering.

'Please...' She reached for him, desperate to have him inside her.

Zack ripped open the condom packet and swiftly applied it, coming back to her in a tangle of limbs. He positioned himself at her entrance, balancing his weight so as not to crush her. 'Tell me if I'm going too fast for you.'

'You're not going fast enough,' Holly said, lifting her hips to receive him.

He put a hand underneath her hip and brought her

up to meet his first thrust. She placed her hands on his buttocks, drawing him down to her aching body, sighing, gasping, almost crying with relief when he entered her slickly, smoothly.

He set a slow pace at first, allowing her time to get used to his thick presence. Her body welcomed him, wrapping around him, pleasure pulsing through her most intimate flesh. He increased his rhythm as if he could no longer control the urges rushing through him. The same urges rushing through Holly. Hot rushes that sent tongues of fire to every corner and crevice of her body.

His breathing became laboured, his hold on her tightening, his pace almost frantic. It was magic, dark wicked magic to have him pumping inside her. But it wasn't quite enough to get her to the summit. As if he could read her body, he slipped a hand between them and began to caress her swollen flesh. The sensations began to ripple through her, giant swamping sensations that made her aware of nothing but what her body was feeling. Feelings she hadn't felt before. Not like this. Not with this powerful rush that swept her into a vortex and spun her around in a dizzying whirlpool before tossing her out the other side, breathless and blissfully sated.

Zack's release followed on the tail of hers, his body driving into her with increasing urgency, his breath hot and fast against her neck. He let out an animal-like groan that made her skin lift in a shiver.

Had she really done that to him? Made him feel the same heart-stopping pleasure he had made her feel?

'Oh, my God…' Holly flung her head back against the pillows. 'That was…amazing.'

Zack smiled and brushed some wayward hair back off her face. 'You were amazing.'

She placed her hand against his chest, close to where his heart was thumping as erratically as hers. She kept her gaze down, focusing on the flat dark circle of his nipple. 'Zack?'

He brought her chin up, meshing his gaze with hers. 'What's troubling you?' There was concern in his expression. Concern and tenderness she hadn't expected to see.

She moistened her lips, tasting where he had been, and another wave of longing swept through her. 'I've never been able to come during oral sex. I used to always pretend to get it over with. But with you…it was so natural. Almost as easy as breathing.'

He leaned forward to press a soft kiss to her mouth. 'You're a very sensual woman. I've been having wicked dreams about your body from the moment I met you.'

Holly traced her finger down the length of his sternum. 'Why me? I mean, I'm not like your usual type.'

'I didn't know I had a type.' His smile was crooked. 'Was I that predictable?'

She pretended to purse her lips. 'I guess you're

used to having anyone you like. You're rich. Handsome. Charming. Good in bed.'

He placed a warm hand on her belly, his gaze teasing. 'Only good?'

She shivered under his light touch. 'Amazing. Awesome. Spectacular.'

He drew a circle on her stomach, making every cell of her body shudder in reaction. 'Some of the sex I've had hasn't been as good as this.'

'I find that hard to believe.'

He brushed a tendril of hair away from her face. 'Why?'

She could feel herself drowning in the deep sapphire sea of his gaze. 'You're so good at seduction. You made me want you from the first moment you looked at me. How did you *do* that?'

He smiled and cupped one of her breasts with his hand. 'It wasn't anything I did. It was what we did. The chemistry we have. I felt it as soon as I saw you. I knew we'd be dynamite together.'

Holly only hoped her involvement with him wouldn't blow up in her face. It was dangerous to let her guard down, but how could she resist this magic? The magic of his hand on her breast, his legs tangled with hers, her body still twitching and tingling from where his had thrust. He had warned her against falling in love with him and she was determined to heed that warning. She had no intention of falling in love with him. Falling in lust was okay. More than okay. Lust, she could handle.

Love, not so much.

Zack's mouth came down on hers in a blistering kiss that made the hairs on her scalp tingle at the roots. His tongue swept over her lower lip before entering her mouth, teasing her tongue into a dance. He made a deep murmuring sound, a sound of pleasure and approval, his hand going to her hip to draw her body closer.

Holly reached down to stroke him, her fingers moving up and down his shaft, delighting in the way his sounds of pleasure intensified. She slithered down his body, pressing kisses to his ridged abdomen. His skin was warm and scented with soap and a hint of male sweat—an intoxicating combination that thrilled her senses. She poked her tongue into the shallow whorl of his belly button, a part of her shocked at how natural it felt to be pleasuring him in such a way. She went lower, trailing her tongue over the section between his belly button and his erection, teasing him with her closeness, with her brazenness.

'You're killing me.' His voice was a raw thread of sound, shredded by his ragged breathing.

Holly circled his tip with her tongue, tasting his pre-ejaculatory fluid. She lifted her head to glance at him from beneath her lashes, a sexy sultry look she hadn't thought herself capable of before. 'Do you want me to stop?'

His hands gripped the bedcover with tight fists. 'You don't have to do this...'

'I want to.' Holly bent her head and opened her mouth over him, taking him in inch by inch, feeling his shudders against the walls of her mouth. It was the most intimate thing she had ever done and yet she felt as if it was the most natural thing in the world to pleasure him as he had pleasured her.

He lay back against the pillows, drawing her head down against his heaving chest, his hand stroking her head like he was soothing a child. 'You'll have to give me a minute to recover.' He turned his head to press a kiss to the top of hers. 'Where did you learn to do that?'

'Not from my exes.' Holly propped herself up beside him, some of her hair falling forward to tickle his chest. She swept it back over her shoulder. 'I never wanted to do it. It revolted me, to be perfectly honest.'

He frowned. 'Then why do it to me if you feel that way? I wouldn't have pressured you.'

She smoothed away his frown with her finger. 'You have this strange effect on me. You make me want to do things I've never done before.'

He rolled her over until she was beneath him, his arms on either side of her head caging her. He brushed her lips with his. 'Likewise. Pretending to be engaged being a case in point.'

Holly lifted her hand to his head, toying with

his hair, running it through her fingers. 'It's kind of sweet how you wanted to help your father by pretending to be in a steady relationship, but aren't you worried about what comes after? When we end it?'

Something moved at the back of his gaze, a fleeting shadow, a ghost of guilt. 'I'm hoping by then I'll have convinced my father I'm capable of more than a run of one-night stands.'

Holly ran her finger down the square line of his jaw from his ear to his chin and back again. 'What's the longest you've been in a relationship?'

'Six weeks.'

'Who ended it? You or her?'

His eyes became shuttered, his expression tightening as if she had touched on a nerve. 'I don't set out to deliberately hurt people, Holly.' He moved away and sat up with his back to her, his hands resting on the bed either side of his legs.

'I wasn't suggesting you did.'

He rose from the bed and picked up his underwear from the floor, stepping into it and turning back to face her. 'I'd better go. I've got court in the morning.'

Holly pulled the bedcovers up to cover her nakedness, suddenly feeling exposed. Vulnerable. 'When will I see you again?' *Damn it.* She sounded like a clingy girlfriend. 'I thought we were going to have dinner?'

'Maybe another night. I'll call you.' He retrieved

his trousers from the floor, put them on and then shrugged himself into his shirt, leaving most of the buttons undone. He raked a hand through his tousled hair and then let out a long breath, his tense shoulders dropping. 'Hey…' His voice had lost its hard edge and a softer light shone in his gaze.

Holly tried to smile but it fell short of the mark. 'I'm sorry, but I'm kind of hoping this wasn't a one-nighter.'

He came back over to the bed and sat alongside her stretched-out legs. He placed a hand on one of her knees and gave it a reassuring squeeze. 'It's not.' He slid his hand up her thigh and she shuddered with another wave of longing. He leaned down to press a lingering kiss to her lips and she wound her arms around his neck, wishing he didn't have to leave but too frightened to ask him to stay in case he said no.

Zack cupped her face, his fingers gliding under the tresses of her hair, making her skin shiver in re-action. 'I want you.' His midnight-blue gaze pulsed with lust, the same lust she could feel vibrating in her body.

Holly traced around his mouth and down his chin with her finger, his stubble as rough as sandpaper. 'It's a bit scary how much I want you…' Her voice was whisper soft and she wondered if she was re-vealing too much by speaking so honestly, so un-guardedly.

He smiled a slow smile that set off a diamond glint

in his eyes. He brought his mouth back down to hers, leaving just enough room for breath. 'It scares the hell out of me how much I want you too.' And then he covered her mouth with his.

CHAPTER SIX

ZACK WOKE WITH his arms around Holly and her hair tickling his face. He glanced at his watch and inwardly groaned. He'd planned to leave hours ago. The sun was peeking through the curtains with bright accusing eyes. So much for his plan to go home before things got too cosy and domestic. They had made love again and then Holly had fixed them a makeshift meal, which they had eaten over a bottle of wine, and then they had gone straight back to bed to make love once more.

He didn't normally spend the night at a lover's place. There was something almost too intimate about it. He was fine with a lover staying over at his house because he could signal when it was time to leave. He liked to be in control of who came and went and how long they stayed.

But somehow with Holly he'd relaxed his rules, which made him wonder if he was walking a fine line. Much finer than he'd planned.

Holly made a soft murmuring sound and stretched

like a cute sleepy kitten. She opened her eyes and winced against the punishing sunlight. 'Ouch. Surely it's not time to get up yet?'

One of her smooth legs bumped against his and desire shot through him like a sniper's bullet. Last night those sexy legs had been wrapped tightly around his waist as he'd driven them both to paradise. He couldn't remember enjoying sex more than with her. Before her, sex was sex. A physical need he satisfied when the opportunity arose.

But with Holly there was a different energy about it, an exciting electric energy that made his body tingle for hours afterwards.

He brushed the tendrils of hair away from her face, bringing his mouth down to hers, losing himself in the pillowy softness of her lips. How could she taste so sweet this early in the morning, or had his taste buds been hijacked? He could have kissed her for hours. Days. He couldn't get enough of her lips moving with breathless urgency against his. He drove his tongue through the seam of her mouth, his groin fizzing and firing and furious with lust as her dancing tongue met his. He groaned against her mouth, need spiralling through him like a red-hot tide. Had he ever wanted anyone as much as her? It was stampeding through his body, giant stomping and galloping footsteps of need.

She made a soft sound against his lips, her hands coming up to play with his hair. God, how he loved it when she did that. It made his scalp tingle when she pulled at the strands in little tugging and releasing movements.

He slid his hand up to cradle the weight of her breast. She had such silky-soft skin, as unblemished as a pearl, her rosy nipple peaking in arousal. He brought his mouth to her breast, licking and stroking the cherry-red flesh surrounding her nipple. He flicked his tongue over her tight nipple and she whimpered in delight. He could smell the scent of her body, the fresh spring flowers overlaid with a hint of musk—his musk and hers, the sexy combination of their bodies making him rock-hard. Painfully rock-hard.

He kissed his way down her ribcage, taking his time to pleasure her with his lips and tongue, enjoying the sound of her breathless gasps. He dipped the tip of his tongue into the cave of her belly button and then went lower to the heart of her. She opened to him like an exotic orchid and he pleasured her with his tongue. She came apart and he felt her buck and thrash under his caress and he thought he had never felt or witnessed anything so damn sexy.

When her storm was over, he came back over her with his weight balanced on his arms. His erection was pounding with the need to let go. He wondered if he'd ever felt so hot for a woman. He kissed her hard on the mouth, lifting his head to look into her glazed-with-ecstasy gaze. 'Hold that thought—I need to get a condom.' He moved off the bed and fished a condom out of his wallet. He was down to the last one and he was struck with the realisation—the scary realisation—he would have made love to her even if he had run out. Another rule he never broke. Never. Not with anyone, and yet here he was tempted to cross yet another line he had never crossed before.

Zack came back to her, gathered her in his arms and she placed her hand on him, stroking and squeezing him until he was ready to blow. He laid her back and entered her with a deep thrust that made her gasp and him groan. Her hands gripped him by the buttocks, urging him on with breathless sounds of delight. He'd had enthusiastic lovers before, but no one matched him like Holly. Her fevered response to his touch, to his body made him feel more of a man than he'd felt with anyone else. It took the experience to another level— an intense level of thrill and excitement.

He could feel his orgasm approaching—a thunderous rush of sensations that drove every thought out of his head. He brought his hand down to the swollen heart of her, caressing her into a tumultuous release that he could feel in tight spasms against his length, triggering his own earth-shattering, planet-dislodging release.

His breathing gradually slowed, his limbs feeling so loose it was as if all the bones had been removed. A wave of lassitude, a feeling of such peace, suddenly swept over him…

* * *

After a few minutes Holly nudged him gently. 'Don't you have to be at work?'

He swore and lifted himself up on his arms, pausing only to plant a kiss on her mouth before he leapt off the bed and grabbed his clothes. 'Sorry to love you and leave you, but I've got to dash if I'm going to make court in time. I have to go home, shower, change and run through my client's brief.'

Holly slipped on her bathrobe and, tying the ends around her waist, followed him out of the bedroom. She was going to be shockingly late too, but at least Jane would fill in for her. 'Thanks for dinner and… you know…everything.'

He smiled and came back over to kiss her. Then he straightened, his expression flickering with something before he asked, 'Can you take a few days off work? I know it's short notice but I have a conference in Paris Monday to Friday next week. We could fly over for the weekend so we have a couple of days together before the conference starts.'

Paris. The City of Love. She would have to get Jane to cover for her but at least Leanne and Taylor were back on deck now that their colds had cleared. Holly wasn't sure her face was wide enough to contain her smile. 'I'd love to come.'

'I'll pick you up this evening around six,' he said. 'Will that give you enough time to get ready?'

She would make time. 'Sure. I'll get Jane to fill in for me at the shop.'

He left a short time later, the flat feeling horribly empty without his presence. He made it seem less like a boring little bedsit and more like an exotic boudoir. She could still smell him on her skin—the citrus and leather and musky scent that reminded her of all the intimate things they had done to each other. She could feel the slight pull of her inner muscles. Every step she took was a heady reminder of the pleasure he had given her. Pleasure she couldn't wait to experience again.

A weekend in Paris with him before his conference started sounded amazing. She would have him to herself in the most romantic city in the world.

Careful. You're not meant to be falling in love with him.

Holly ignored the prod of her conscience. Her uptight overcontrolling conscience had no right interfering. She wasn't falling in love with him. She was enjoying having a fling—an exhilarating, wickedly sexy fling with the most attractive man she'd ever met.

She knew exactly what she was doing. She had it under control. She was a young woman of close to thirty who was discovering her sensual side, the side that had lain dormant until now. She was more aware of her body than she had ever been before. It was glowing inside and out. She felt more confident in her body, was amazed by its ability to give and receive such mind-blowing pleasure.

That could only be a good thing, couldn't it?

'Oh. My. God,' Sabrina said when she came into Holly's workroom on her lunch break. 'You've slept with him, haven't you?'

Holly frowned. 'How can you possibly tell?'

'You've got stubble rash, for one thing.' Sabrina pointed to Holly's chin. 'And you've got a certain glow about you I've never seen on you before.'

Holly didn't see the point in denying it. 'I'm supposed to be engaged to him so why wouldn't I sleep with him?'

'How was it?'

'Amazing.' Holly suppressed a shiver, just as she did every time she thought of Zack's lovemaking. 'The best sex I've ever had. Not only that, he's taking me to Paris for the weekend before he has to attend a conference next week. He's asked me to stay the whole time with him.'

'Uh-oh.' Sabrina pulled up a stool and sat at the workbench.

'What's with the "uh-oh"?' Holly said. 'I know what I'm doing. I've got it under control.'

Sabrina shook her head at her. 'You haven't taken a weekend off work in eons, let alone a whole flipping week. You are *so* going to fall in love with him.'

Holly squared her shoulders. 'I am not.'

Sabrina leaned her elbows on the workbench and sighed. 'Don't mind me—I'm just ridiculously jealous. I can't remember the last time I had amazing sex. But I think it might've been with myself.'

'Maybe if you weren't so fussy, you'd have more luck with dating.'

'I don't see why I should apologise for having high standards when it comes to the men I date,' Sabrina said. 'If I don't like them after the first date, why would I go on a second one?'

'Have you ever been on more than one date with a man?'

Sabrina lowered her gaze and sighed. 'No...'

'Maybe you should rethink the Max Firbank thing. As least you know each other, which is a whole lot less scary than dating a stranger.'

Sabrina gave her the slitted eye. 'What is this sudden obsession with Max Firbank? I've told you what I think about him.'

'I know, but remember that family function you asked me to attend with you a few weeks ago? I saw Max watching you all evening.'

'So?' Sabrina's scowl would have made a three-year-old proud. 'He only does that so he can witness me spill a drink or bump into something.'

'Maybe, but when you got up to dance with one of your brother's friends, Max downed his drink in one gulp and walked out of the room with a brooding frown on his face.'

Sabrina's expression looked puzzled. 'Did he?'

'Yep. And I bet if you dated Max Firbank you'd have amazing sex.'

'I wouldn't sleep with him if he paid me.'

'I'm pretty sure men as gorgeous-looking as Max Firbank don't need to pay for sex.'

Sabrina hopped down off the stool in an abrupt manner that said 'subject closed'. Even the way her feet hit the floor sounded like a punctuation mark. 'I'd better get back to the studio. I have a couple of brides coming in for fittings. That reminds me—have things picked up for you now you're "engaged"—' she did the air quote thing with her fingers '—to Mr Amazing Sex Zack Knight?'

'Yes. The phone has barely stopped. And my website's had more hits in the last twenty-four hours than it has for the last month. I've got a couple of last-minute bookings for May and June and July, plus I've got three weddings booked in for August and four for September. Big ones too.'

Sabrina smiled and gave Holly a high five. 'You go, girl. You're on fire.'

Holly was so on fire she could feel it smouldering deep in her core. A smoking-hot week in Paris with Zack and she was sure to combust into flames.

CHAPTER SEVEN

ZACK GOT THROUGH his day's work with his usual brisk efficiency, but one corner of his mind kept drifting to the amazing sex he'd had with Holly last night. He had never enjoyed someone's company as much as he enjoyed hers. She was cute and sweet and so damn sexy he felt like a horny teenager. He couldn't get enough of her. Her touch sent shivers over his flesh, electric shivers that made him realise he had never been with a woman who had excited him more.

He'd thought of nothing but her all day. Every time he had a spare moment, his mind would drift to how it had felt to have her in his arms last night and in the early hours of the morning. His middle-aged secretary, Carol, had laughed at him when he hadn't heard her ask him something about a client. He'd been too preoccupied, staring into space, thinking about how Holly's mouth felt on him. Carol smiled knowingly at him as if he were some lovesick fool who didn't know the difference between love and lust.

He was in lust, not love. He wanted Holly like he'd wanted no other woman. That wasn't love. It was chemistry. Damn great chemistry. Awesome chemistry and he was going to enjoy it while it lasted.

Because it wouldn't last.

It never did.

It would burn out after a time, just as it had with his other lovers. He would gradually become bored, his body not so excited any more. It happened every time and he didn't expect this time to be any different. This week in Paris would prove it. It was the longest he would have spent with anyone in years. He'd be lucky to get to the middle of next week without the shine wearing off his enthusiasm for her.

Zack ducked home to his house in Chelsea to pack a weekend bag and was about to leave to pick up Holly when his phone rang with a call from his father. His stomach nosedived. He loved his dad but cancelling his week with Holly was out of the question. Way out of the question. 'Dad, how are things?'

'Guess what? I've met someone.'

Zack had heard it all before. His dad had met lots of women over the years but none of them ever measured up to Zack's mother. They often looked like her—that seemed to be the pattern his dad followed—slim stylish blondes—but they never *were* his mother. And so the heaven and hell cycle would begin all over again. 'That's…nice.' He glanced at his watch and suppressed a groan.

'I know you're probably thinking it will end like all the others, but I've known Kayla for years. We went to school together but we lost touch after I married your mother. She's a widow now and she lives only a few doors away from me.'

'That's really great. I'm happy for you, Dad. Really happy.'

'Maybe you and Holly could have dinner with Kayla and I sometime,' his dad said. 'A double date.'

'Sounds like a plan. I'll organise something the week after next. I'm off to Paris with Holly this weekend for a few days.'

'Paris, huh?' His dad whistled through his teeth. 'Nice work, son. The most romantic city in the world.'

So far so good with convincing his dad he was on the straight and narrow. 'Yep, I'm really looking forward to spending some quality time with her.'

'I can't tell you how happy I am to see you finally settling down,' his dad said. 'Have you set a date for the wedding yet?'

What was with his dad's obsession with him getting married? *Sheesh.* 'Not yet, but you'll be the first to know.'

Zack ended the call a short time later and frowned, guilt gnawing at his guts. He might have fooled his dad that he was engaged, but what was he going to say when he found out there wasn't going to be a wedding?

Holly left work as early as she could so she could rush to the shops and find some new outfits to take on her week away to Paris with Zack. She hadn't shopped for new clothes in so long and took way too much time trying to choose between two gorgeous dresses, so in the end she bought both. She picked up a few casuals and a new pair of shoes, because who didn't need a new pair of shoes? She managed to squeeze in a quick manicure as her hands bore the brunt of working with flowers day in, day out. She looked at the shiny dark blue polish and thought of Zack's midnight gaze and how it simmered with lust when he looked at her.

She dashed back to her flat and showered and dried her hair, leaving it in a cloud of curls around her shoulders. She stood back to look at her reflection, pleased with how her blue dress—the exact colour of Zack's eyes—hugged her figure in all the right places. Places that even now were tingling at the thought of his hands moving over them.

The doorbell rang and Holly took a breath to calm her overexcited nerves before she opened it. Zack was standing there, dressed in dark blue denim jeans, a white shirt and a navy blazer. His hair looked like it had been recently combed with his fingers and his features looked strained, tense as if he'd had a tough day at the office. He stepped over the threshold, closed the door and took her in his arms and planted a warm, lingering kiss on her mouth.

He pulled back after a dizzying moment to smile at her but she noticed it didn't quite reach his eyes. 'Ready?'

Holly felt something slip inside her chest. Was he having second thoughts about their trip to Paris? 'Is everything all right?'

He released a short breath. 'Sorry I'm a bit late.' He picked up her bag that was waiting by the door. 'I got held up with a call from my dad.'

Holly recalled how he'd told her that he had to give his father extra support from time to time. Was that why he looked so tense? 'Is he okay?'

'He's in love.' A flicker of cynicism rippled across his face. 'Again.'

'And that's a bad thing?'

'It never lasts.' He held the door open for her so they could leave.

Holly followed him out to the car and waited until they were on their way before she continued the conversation. She glanced at his frowning expression as he started the engine. 'But maybe this time your dad has found The One.'

He sent her a sideways glance. 'I thought you didn't believe in that fairy-tale crap?' His tone had a sharp edge that unexpectedly stung.

Holly pressed her lips together and turned to

look out of the passenger window. She didn't want to argue with him. This was supposed to be a romantic getaway. She didn't want it to be spoilt with bickering.

'Hey.' Zack ran a hand underneath her hair and turned her head to look at him. 'Sorry, sweetie. I'm in a foul mood. Forgive me?'

She gave a tremulous smile. 'It's okay...'

His fingers began to caress the back of her neck, making her shiver in reaction. His eyes were so dark she couldn't make out his pupils. 'I've spent a lot of my life worrying about my father.' He let out a long jagged sigh. 'I want to believe he'll be happy, that this time he'll find what he's looking for in a partner, but so far it's always ended the same way. He gets shattered when a woman ends it. Absolutely shattered.'

Holly touched his face, stroking her hand down his late-in-the-day stubble. 'Some people feel more deeply than others. They get hurt more often.' *Isn't that the truth?* 'But he's lucky to have you to watch out for him. You're a good person, Zack.'

He leaned closer to cover her mouth in a tender kiss that made her feel unexpectedly emotional. When he pulled back she blinked and turned to the front so he wouldn't see the glisten of moisture in her eyes. But he must have sensed something for he placed a finger beneath her chin and turned her slowly to face him. His eyes moved between each of hers in a back-and-forth motion, a searching motion that made her feel even more exposed and vulnerable. 'Please tell me I haven't made you cry.' His voice was so husky it sounded like it had been dragged over a rough surface.

Holly smiled. 'No, you haven't, but if we miss that flight to Paris, I'll cry buckets.'

'Me too,' he said but he didn't say it with a smile, but with a frown.

They arrived in Paris and caught a cab to the hotel Zack had booked on Rue de Rivoli, overlooking the Jardin des Tuileries, the stunning gardens that were a short walk from the Louvre. Holly felt like she'd stepped into a fairy tale—*there was that pesky word again*—when Zack led her to their luxury suite. The suite was decorated in dove grey and white with occasional touches of black. The grey sofas were plush velvet chesterfields and there was a matching wing chair and an ottoman. The lamp tables were glass, so too the table lampstands and the shades were a bone white that lifted the darker hues of the furniture. The carpet was so deep Holly felt like she was walking on a cloud, but then in a way she was—being here with Zack was every girl's romantic dream.

He had even gone to the trouble of having the room filled with flowers. There were tiny bunches of violets—not just the purple ones, but the much rarer white ones. The roses too were not the tightly budded fragrance-free hothouse ones, but fully blown and heady with the scent of spice and musk and cloves. A tall vase of pink hollyhocks and foxgloves were on a glass-topped sideboard and another shorter vase, spilling over with colourful and fragrant sweet peas, was on a coffee table.

Holly leaned down to smell the sweet peas and gave a sigh of bliss. 'You've really raised the benchmark, Zack. No one will ever be able to top this.'

'Do you like them?'

'I love them. It's like being at work but not.' She picked up the posy of white violets and pressed her nose into their cool fresh sweetness.

Zack uncorked the champagne that was sitting in an ice bucket and handed her a glass. 'You're lucky. Few people can say they love being at work.'

Holly took the glass and clinked it against his. 'Don't you enjoy yours?'

He took a sip of his champagne and rocked his other hand back and forth. 'Yes and no.'

She joined him on one of the velvet sofas, moving one of the scatter cushions to place it behind her back. 'What don't you like about it?'

He stared into the contents of his glass for a moment, a frown between his brows. 'Take today, for instance.' He looked at her. 'I've had this client's divorce dragging out for almost three years. It's costing him a fortune, but he insists on challenging the prenuptial agreement his ex insisted on when they married.' He screwed up his mouth and looked back at his glass. 'Kind of makes me wonder if he only married her for her money.'

'It happens.'

'Yes...' His frown deepened. 'You'd be amazed at how cruel some couples can be to each other. How can people who once claimed to love each other change so much? It doesn't make sense, unless they didn't love each other in the first place.'

'People change,' Holly said. 'Feelings change.' *Wasn't that the truth?* She could feel her feelings undergoing a subtle change. Had done so since the first time he'd kissed her. If she wasn't careful she would be in way over her head. Way, way over her foolish romantic head. Drowning in feelings she wasn't supposed to be feeling as per their agreement. No falling in love.

Zack took another measured sip of his champagne, his frown relaxing. He put his glass down on the nearest lamp table and then took hers and placed it beside his. He picked up a wayward curl of her hair and wound it around his finger. 'Did I tell you how beautiful you look tonight?'

Holly gazed into his night-sky eyes and felt another piece of armour drop away from her heart like petals falling from a rose. She would have to be super careful not to fall in love with him. He was everything she had dreamed of in a partner. Loving, attentive, sensitive and spine tinglingly masculine and sexy. 'You look pretty awesome yourself.' Her voice came out as a whisper. A whisper of longing and need she could no longer suppress.

He gave a slow smile and brought his mouth down to hers, moving his lips in a gentle caress of her mouth that made her blood heat like fire in her veins. Her hands came to rest on the hard wall of his chest, her body listing towards him as if pulled by a magnetic force. Her inner core contracted when his tongue found hers, teasing it into a dance that made her heart race and her skin tighten in anticipation. His hands slid up on either side of her face, cradling her head so he could deepen the kiss. The writhing and tangling of their tongues made her ache for his possession. Ache and ache and ache until she was whimpering and blindly tearing at his clothes.

His hands moved from cradling her head to slipping off her dress. She shivered when he unclipped her bra, his hands warm and gentle as they cupped her sensitive flesh. His thumbs rolled over each of her nipples and then he bent his head and swirled his tongue over her peaked flesh. Darts of longing shot through her body and she gasped when his teeth grazed her in a gentle tiger bite.

Holly went to work on his shirt, almost ripping it from his body and pressing open-mouthed kisses to his chest. Her hands went lower to the proud bulge of his erection and she quickly unfastened his jeans and dipped her hand beneath the fabric of his underwear to claim her prize.

'Bedroom. Now.' Zack pulled her to her feet and led her to the sumptuous bedroom that was decorated in similar tones to the sitting room.

But Holly barely had time to notice her surroundings—all she could concentrate on was the magic of his hands on her body, the raging fire of lust in her body that seemed to be just as ferocious in his. The rest of their clothes were removed and thrown to the floor, underwear discarded like tossed garbage and then bliss as naked flesh met naked flesh.

Zack drove into her with a swift deep thrust that made her moan in sheer pleasure, her body wrapping around him, her legs hooked behind his hips, her hips rising to meet each downward thrust of his. It was a wild coupling, a wild animalistic thrashing of the senses until there was nowhere else to go but heaven. Holly felt herself lift off, her body racked with ecstasy, ripples and waves and floods of release.

His release followed hers and he gave a desperate-sounding groan, his body rocking and shuddering until he was spent. She held him close, listening to the gradual slowing of his breathing, wondering if he had been as stunned by their lovemaking as she was. Had it been this good with his other lovers? Was this run-of-the-mill sex for him? She could feel his essence between her thighs, could smell the musky scent of their aroused bodies.

He suddenly swore, rolled away and sat up, scraping a hand through his hair. Holly lifted herself up on her elbows. 'What's the matter? Did I do something wrong?'

His frown sliced like a knife between his brows. 'I did something wrong.' He got up from the bed and rubbed a hand down his face. He turned and looked at her with such a look of disgust she shrank back against the pillows. 'I didn't protect you.'

Holly realised then what he meant. In the mad rush to make love he hadn't used a condom. 'It's okay. I'm on the pill. I use it to regulate my periods.'

He let out a savage-sounding breath. 'Doesn't matter. I should've used one regardless.'

Holly moistened her suddenly dry lips. 'I hope you're not implying I might be carrying some sort of disease?'

He closed his eyes in a slow blink. 'No.' His tone lost some of its brittle edge. He came back to sit beside her on the rumpled bed. 'No, I'm not implying that at all… It's just I take protection seriously. Always. I never ride bareback.'

'But we're being exclusive and I'm using reliable contraception,' Holly said. 'You don't have to worry about using a condom, not unless you don't plan to be faithful for as long as we're together.'

He flinched at the word *faithful* as if she'd slapped him. 'I saw what my mother's unfaithfulness did to my father. I have never cheated on a partner. If I feel even a mild attraction for someone else, then I do my current partner a favour and tell her it's over.'

Was that what he would do to her? Tell her he was attracted to someone else and then cut her from his life? Holly suddenly realised how much power she had given him—the power to hurt her. The power to break her heart like it had never been broken before. She swallowed a tight restriction in her throat and kept her gaze averted. 'So…you'll tell me when you're ready to move on?' She wished her voice hadn't sounded so thready.

Zack bumped up her chin, meshing his gaze with hers. 'I'm with you right now, Holly. This week is ours, okay?'

But for how long after that? Holly eased out of his hold and tossed her hair back behind her shoulders. 'I might be the one to end it first. I might be the one who feels attracted to someone else.' She lifted her chin another fraction. 'I might get bored.'

His jaw worked for a moment, as if he was biting back a retort, the words backed up behind his tongue like soldiers keen to go into a bloody battle. His eyes contained a dangerous light. A light that warned her she had roused an emotion in him he didn't like feeling. Possibly a feeling he had never felt before—jealousy.

'You could.' His tone was back to brittle, all hard edges and corners. His hands came down either side of her body, trapping her on the bed.

Holly could feel her body preparing itself, the tight clench of her inner core, the prickling sensation coursing over her breasts and belly, the intimate moisture between her legs. Desire so hot and strong it threatened to consume her. To burn her. To scorch her. To destroy her. She couldn't stop herself reaching for him, pulling him down so his mouth crashed against hers in an explosion of lust.

It was a hard kiss, hard and insistent and irresistible. Brutal passion flared between their mouths, stoked by the twin fires of jealousy and defiance. Holly relished in the black magic of it, the way his kiss triggered something feral inside her. No one would ever be able to kiss her like this, like he wanted to devour her. No one could ever make her feel as if she would literally die if he didn't possess her. Her body was twitching, twisting, tortured by rampant need. Her nerves were aching for his touch, her intimate muscles contracting in anticipation of his passionate possession.

How could she ever want anyone more than him?

He pinned her to the bed with his weight, the erotic tangle of their limbs sending her senses into another tailspin. He brought his mouth in a hot kiss to her breast, his lips and tongue caressing her flesh until she was writhing beneath him, wanting more, aching for more. He moved to her other breast, his teeth taking her nipple in a bite just short of pain, the exquisite torture making her fist her hands in his hair, dragging his mouth back to hers.

He turned her so she was on top of him, her legs splayed on either side of his hips, the heart of her so painfully aroused she could feel it pulsating. She took control and mounted him, sinking onto his turgid length with a cry that was almost primal.

He held her by the forearms, his movements within her body strong and forceful, but Holly wanted him that way. He was exactly where she needed him most, the friction of his erection against her swollen clitoris sending her into the stratosphere.

She had barely come out of her orgasm when he flipped her over again, this time so he could enter her from behind. A part of her split from her mind and looked on from above, almost a little shocked at her shamelessly resting on all fours with him holding her hips and thrusting his way to his own release. She had never been all that adventurous with sex in the past. But Zack unlocked something in her, something wild and uncontrollable.

He suddenly gasped and groaned, shook and shuddered and then collapsed, bringing her with him in a hold that was unexpectedly, disarmingly tender given the tumultuous storm of passion they had just shared.

Holly laid her head against his chest, listening to the thud-pitty-thud of his heart. His hand played with her hair, the other rested on the flank of her thigh crossed over his body. She had never been good at post-coital conversation but, after such an earth-shattering experience, what words could ever be adequate? There weren't enough superlatives to cover what she had just experienced. Her body would never be the same. *She* would never be the same.

Zack shifted beneath her splayed limbs, turning her so she was on her back. He smoothed her hair back from her face, his touch so gentle it made her wonder if there was a part of him that was developing feelings for her in spite of his determination not to. His expression was hard to read—inscrutable, unfathomable, and yet with a shadow of something at the edges of his gaze as if he was working hard to keep it that way. 'Are you hungry?' he asked.

Her stomach growled audibly in response and she laughed. 'I'm always hungry. Don't you know that about me by now?'

He gave a ghost of a smile and found another tendril of hair to tuck back behind her ear. 'I love hearing you laugh. It sounds like a tinkling bell.'

Holly wondered if she'd still be able to laugh in a few weeks or months, once their 'engagement' came to an end. But she didn't want to think about that now. For now, she wanted to live in the moment. Wasn't that what all the meditation experts said you had to do? *Stop stressing the small stuff. Enjoy the moment. Live in the now.*

She traced the bridge of his nose with her finger. 'Are you hungry?'

He gave her a smouldering look. 'Starving.'

Somehow Holly knew he wasn't talking about food. She arched one of her eyebrows in mock surprise. 'Not again?'

He smiled and brought his mouth down to just above hers. 'Always.'

CHAPTER EIGHT

LATER THAT NIGHT Zack managed to drag himself out of bed and away from the temptation of Holly's body. It was ridiculously late to be going in search of something to eat, but this was Paris and there was always somewhere open. He found a late-night tapas bar and they shared some food and wine, chatting over inconsequential things as if they'd been together for years.

His body was still recovering from the sensual workout he'd subjected it to. Strike that—*what Holly had subjected it to.* He couldn't resist her. She was like a drug he hadn't realised until now he needed to stay alive. Had he ever felt this alive? It was like he had been tuned to a higher setting. He was noticing things he had never noticed before. Colours, angles of light—even the food and wine tasted different.

He *felt* different.

Zack looked at Holly sitting across from him. She was wearing a navy blue velvet dress that highlighted

her creamy complexion. Her hair was wild about her
shoulders, her mouth still swollen from his kisses.
And yes, the little patch of stubble rash was on her
chin like a brand.

His brand.

He refused to be ashamed about the ferocity of
his lovemaking. She had been with him all the way.
He couldn't remember having more exciting sex. She
met his fire with fire. She stoked the fire within him,
turning it into something wild and uncontrollable.
He had never had sex without a condom before. Not
even when he was a teenager. He had always used
protection. Always. But with Holly he had his guard
down and made love to her without a barrier. It worried him that if he wasn't careful he might lower
other barriers. Barriers he had never intended on
lowering. With anyone.

When she'd said she might be the one to end their
relationship, he'd been triggered by the most appall-
ing jealousy. He had never felt jealous before. Why
would he? He had never invested himself emotionally
in a relationship. He had always kept his distance.
Kept his guard up. But somehow with Holly he had
lowered his guard and allowed her close.

Too close.

Dangerously close.

Holly put down her half-empty wine glass. 'That's
it. I'm done. I'll be dancing on the tables to ABBA
if I drink another mouthful.'

Zack reached for her hand and smiled. 'Do you like dancing?'

Her eyes lit up like beacons. 'I love dancing.'

He rose from the table and drew her to her feet and into the circle of his arms. The band was playing a romantic ballad that somehow suited his mood. She looked up at him with dreamy eyes, or maybe that was his vision playing tricks on him—some of those settings on her personality, on his perception tampered with, without his awareness—without his permission.

But then, with a soft sigh, she settled closer against him, her lush curves against his hard planes, her cheek resting on his chest, her arms around his waist as if she never wanted to let him go.

He hadn't realised until now that dancing was a little like making love. Some couples looked like they belonged together, their bodies meshing, moulding, moving as one entity. His body moved in time with hers, the rhythm of the music somehow matching the rhythm of their bodies. Slow, sensual, sexy.

Holly glanced up at him and smiled, her eyes as sparkling bright as the diamond ring on her finger. 'Normally when I dance with someone I tread on their toes.'

Zack pulled her closer, right up against his painfully tight erection. 'It's not my toes you're treading on right now.'

Her cheeks flushed a delicate pink. 'Thanks for bringing me to Paris. I'm having an amazing time.'

He pressed a kiss to the middle of her forehead. 'So am I.'

They left the bar a short time later and walked hand in hand along the riverbank of the Seine. It was a cool night with a light breeze that wrinkled the water like crushed silk, but Holly felt warm from Zack's company. And possibly from the amount of alcohol she'd consumed. It was hard to tell if she was tipsy from the delicious wine and champagne or because he was so the most attentive and romantic man she had ever met. Dancing in his arms had felt as amazing as making love with him. There was the same natural rhythm and motion as if they'd been dancing together for years.

They got back to their hotel in the early hours of the morning and, although Holly should have been tired, instead she turned in his arms as soon as the door of their suite closed. His mouth came down on hers in a gentle kiss that soon turned into something else, something greedy and passionate that refused to be contained. His tongue drove through the seam of her lips, tangling with hers in a combative duel that made the fine hairs on the back of her neck stand up and a storm of need gather between her thighs.

He walked her backwards to the bedroom, blindly

skirting around furniture, almost at one point knocking over one of the lamps. He began working on her clothes as she worked at his, tossing them to one side like sheets of paper ruthlessly ripped off a gift.

But then he was a gift—a gift to her senses. Her senses had been dead before him. Deadened by boredom. No one had ever made her feel this level of arousal. This spine-tingling level of thrilling *aliveness* that made her blood sing through her veins and her heart run like a supercar in her chest.

Zack pressed her down to the bed, coming over her with his body, his mouth a hot liquid fire on her breasts, on her sternum, on her quivering belly. She sucked in a breath as he went lower, his mouth on her where she throbbed and ached the most. He stroked her with his tongue up and down and in tiny circles until she was teetering on a vertiginous cliff. Her back arched off the bed as the orgasm smashed into her, making her shudder and moan and thrash beneath him.

He waited only long enough for her to catch her breath and he was inside her, driving into her with breathless gasps and deep guttural groans that signalled the thundering approach of his release. He tensed all over, his grip on her wrists somewhere in that hazy area between pleasure and pain. And then he let finally himself go, letting out a low desperate-sounding growl that made her skin lift in a shiver as the shudders racked his body, leaving him spent and useless in her arms.

Holly moved her hands up and down his back and shoulders in light massaging movements, her erratic breathing gradually slowing to keep time with his. She had never felt so physically close to someone. There was gorgeous symmetry to their lovemaking, a pattern, a beautiful, sensual choreography that was almost beyond description. It was as if in a parallel universe their bodies were delicately synchronised, recognising the other as its perfect mate.

She closed her eyes and listened to him breathing, her senses sated, every muscle deliciously relaxed. The sounds of Paris at night faded into the background, her worries about the future—her future with Zack—a muffled white noise at the back of her brain...

On Saturday morning, after a shower together and a light breakfast, Zack took Holly on a walk through the streets of Paris. They walked hand in hand as they visited the Louvre—it was more of a whistle-stop tour, as it would have taken them most of the day to see everything. Holly stood in front of the *Mona Lisa*, with her mercurial expression and wondered if people looking at *her* could see how Zack made her feel. She could feel his warm, strong fingers against hers, his body with its familiar smell of citrus and leather teasing her nostrils and delighting her senses. Every time he met her gaze she felt a tug deep in her belly, his dark eyes glinting with erotic promise, triggering a twinge of her intimate muscles.

'What time does your conference start on Monday?' Holly asked as they were walking along the Seine later that afternoon.

'Registration is at eight. The first plenary session is at nine.'

She glanced up at him. 'Are you giving a paper?'

'Yep.'

'What's it about?'

'Custodial arrangements.'

Holly stopped walking to look at him. 'Because of what happened to you when your mother left your father?'

He shrugged. 'A little, I guess.' He continued walking, taking her along with him as if keen to move away from the subject.

'What other topics have you spoken on?'

'I did one the year before on using forensic accounting to keep track of fathers who claim to have no income to support their children in the event of a divorce.' He let out a jaded-sounding sigh. 'You'd be amazed at the lengths some super-wealthy men will go to to avoid paying child support, hiding money in offshore accounts and so on.'

Holly couldn't help thinking what a great father Zack would make. His sense of justice was so strong, so admirable. She was ashamed now of how badly she had misjudged him when she'd first met him. His reputation as a celebrity divorce lawyer had made her picture him as only in it for the money, but she could see now that nothing could be further from the truth. He was passionate about doing the right thing by his clients.

'It's kind of sad you don't want to get married yourself and have a family,' she said after a short pause.

'Why's that?' His tone had a guarded edge to it.

'Because I think you'd make a great dad, given how close you are to yours.'

His hand released hers as if her touch had burned him. 'I hope this isn't leading where I think it's leading.'

Holly knew she had crossed a line but hadn't been able to stop herself in time. 'I don't know why you have to be so prickly about a throwaway comment.'

'But was it a throwaway comment?' Cynicism sharpened his gaze.

'Of course it was,' Holly said. 'You surely don't think I want to change the rules of our engagement?'

He studied her for a pulsing moment. 'This week is not a promise of a future. I didn't ask you to come with me for any other reason than to hang out and have some fun together.' He released a short breath and added, 'And to convince my father I'm not just a one-night stand playboy.'

Holly raised her chin. 'It's no fun with you glaring

at me like that. If you're going to be so prickly, then maybe I should go home and leave you to it.'

After a tense moment he relaxed his features and gave a crooked smile. 'You're right. I'm being a jerk.' He took her hand and entwined his fingers with hers. 'I know it looks like I'm close to my dad but, to be honest, I've always felt like the adult in our relationship. It gets a little wearing, especially when he's in a new relationship. I can't help bracing myself for the fallout when it's over.'

'Maybe this new relationship will last,' Holly said. 'Have you met your dad's new partner?'

'Not yet, but apparently he's known her for years, even before he met my mother.'

Holly stroked the back of his hand with her fingers. 'Your dad is lucky to have you to watch out for him. But do you think he relies *too* much on your support?'

Zack looped her arm through his and continued walking along the footpath, his brow slightly furrowed. 'I think it's a pattern we've slipped into. I go into parent mode. He goes into helpless child mode.' He sent her a sideways smile. 'Hey, why the heck are you a wedding florist? You would've made a great relationships counsellor.'

Holly gave him a playful shoulder bump. 'Yeah, like I'm an expert at relationships with two broken engagements under my belt.'

Zack wound his arm around her waist and gave

her a gentle squeeze. 'I'm sure they weren't your fault.'

Holly chewed her lip for a beat or two. 'I think I was in both of those relationships for the wrong reasons. But I've learnt my lesson.' *Or at least I hope I have.*

'What were your reasons?'

She looked away, not sure she could face him and the truth about herself at the same time. 'I don't know… I guess I wanted to belong to someone…' She chanced a quick glance at him and found him looking at her with a thoughtful expression. 'I admire my parents so much for their relationship. They have each other's backs no matter what. But I chose men I couldn't rely on.' She frowned. 'What does that say about me?'

Zack brushed his knuckles beneath her chin to lift her gaze. 'It says more about them than it does about you.'

But what did her relationship with Zack say about her now? He wasn't signing up for the long-term so there was no point hoping this fling could turn into something else. The something else she wanted so badly it was like an ache. The more time she spent with him the deeper the ache became, burrowing into every crevice and corner of her heart. He was so different from her exes. He was hard-working and dependable, strong and trustworthy. He made her feel special. He listened to her as if he found every word that came out of her mouth profoundly interesting. He made exquisite love to her, always making sure her needs were satisfied before his own.

He made her feel...*loved*.

Holly mentally scoffed at the thought of him loving her. Paris must be really getting to her if she was imagining Zack was in love with her. Although... the way he kept looking at her with his eyes all soft and warm and that sexy smile that made her feel like the most desirable woman on the planet surely must count for something?

On Sunday morning, after a long and sexy sleep-in, Zack led her to a café that overlooked the Seine. They sat at an outside table and ordered coffees and patisseries they selected from an array of colourful and artful delicacies on display in a glass cabinet.

Holly had just about finished her utterly delicious strawberry-and-cream-cheese pastry with toffee glaze and was trying not to stare at Zack's lemon-and-lime tart, which so far he hadn't touched. He took occasional sips of his black espresso, his expression like that of an indulgent uncle taking a much-favoured niece out for a treat.

Holly put her cake fork down and sighed in pleasure. 'Seriously? That was to die for.'

He pushed his tart towards her. 'Do you want mine?'

'Don't you want it?'

He smiled. 'I'll get far more pleasure watching you eat it.'

Holly could feel her cheeks going as red as the strawberry coulis on her plate. 'I have a sweet tooth, so shoot me.'

'It was one of the first things I noticed about you. You were the only woman at Kendra's divorce party going back for seconds at the dessert table.'

'Yeah, well, that's me all right.' Holly's tone was self-deprecating with a side order of shame. 'A glutton for punishment. That's probably why I've got two broken engagements behind me. I don't learn from my mistakes. I just barge right back in and make another one.' Like the one she was in the middle of making now. How could she have thought she could have a fling with him without involving her emotions? She wasn't ready to call it love. Not yet. But something was happening to the armour around her heart and it terrified her. She felt connected to Zack in a way she had never felt with anyone else. The way he looked at her melted her bones. The way he touched her made her flesh tingle from head to foot. The longer she spent with him the more dangerous it would be. But how could she bring herself to end it before it went too far?

Before *she* went too far?

Zack placed his cup back on its saucer and then reached for her hand. 'Holly.' There was a note of warning in his tone and a hint of pressure where his hand was anchoring hers to the table. 'What we're doing isn't a mistake. We're helping each other. You're getting your business back on track and I'm helping my dad. And we're having a good time while doing it—aren't we?'

Holly stretched her lips into a smile. 'Yep. An awesome time.' The best time ever. A time she would always look back on as a landmark in her life. A turning point where she had discovered the passion she was capable of, a passion she had never experienced with anyone else.

And probably wouldn't experience with anyone else.

No. *Definitely* wouldn't experience with anyone else.

Zack watched Holly eat his citrus tart, his thoughts like wrestling monkeys in his head. Of course it wasn't a mistake to indulge in a pretend engagement with her. They each stood to gain by it. Hadn't she told him her business had already picked up? And look at his dad, happy for the first time in months. His dad's new relationship might not last—it could well turn out as bitter as the rest—but he'd noticed a different quality in his dad's voice, a quality he had never heard before. Hope.

Zack was not out to hurt Holly, far from it. He had wanted her from the first moment he'd seen her at the divorce party. Kendra had talked about Holly

to him, telling him she was a man-hater after being
jilted twice, and he'd smiled to himself, confident
he could win her over. But he'd been unprepared for
how attractive he would find her. Her vibrancy, her
energy, her wilfulness and defiance had sparked his
interest in a way it had never been sparked before.
He had felt it on a cellular level. He still couldn't
believe how much he'd lowered his guard. Making
love with her without a condom involved a heap of
trust. Loads and loads of trust. Trust was not something he handed out too casually. He was cautious
and cynical by nature and yet he had relaxed his
guard because he'd been blown away by his fever-
ish attraction to her. It secretly terrified him how
attracted he was. It wasn't like anything he'd experienced in the past.

There was lust and there was *Lust*.

He could feel it stirring in his body now—the
tingle in his groin when her gaze met his across the
table. The fizzing at the base of his spine when her
hand slipped into his. The tick of his pulse when
she smiled at him. Would he ever get sick of seeing
her dazzling smile? It was like sunshine breaking
through dark brooding clouds.

A toddler tottered towards their table and tripped
over Holly's tote bag where it was lying on the floor
next to the table. The child fell to her little hands and
knees and promptly let out a piercing wail. Holly
helped the little girl back to her feet just as her harried

mother came rushing over, carrying a newborn baby along one arm, her nappy bag, shopping bag and purse bundled over the other.

'I'm so sorry,' the young mother said to Holly, who, in Zack's opinion, had done an excellent job of averting a full-blown tantrum from the little girl.

'That's okay.' Holly smiled. 'She's a little pet, isn't she?' She leaned down to speak to the child. 'What's your name, sweetie?'

The little girl had popped her thumb in her mouth and spoke around it. 'Ibee.'

'Ivy,' the young mother said with a rueful smile. 'She gave up her thumb months ago but she's been sucking it again because of the new baby.'

Zack had thought Holly had drooled in front of the patisserie counter but it was nothing next to how she looked at the blue bundle of the baby. Her features melted into maternal longing and he saw her place her hand against her heart as if it had suddenly pained her. 'Oh, isn't he adorable? How old is he?'

'Three weeks,' the young woman said. 'I really shouldn't come out with both of them without help but it was such a nice day and Ivy gets bored being home all day. My husband is on call this weekend. He's a doctor. An anaesthetist. We're here for a couple of years, but we plan to go back to England when Ivy starts school.'

Little Ivy looked shyly at Zack, her thumb still

stuck in her rosebud mouth. He winked at the little girl and she smiled around her thumb and then pushed her face into her mother's legs.

'Would you like me to hold the baby while you sort out your bags?' Holly said, obviously noticing how the young mother was struggling to keep everything in order.

'Oh, would you? Thanks ever so much.'

The baby was duly handed over and Zack watched as Holly cradled the infant against her with a soft, melting look in her eyes. And apparently conscious of not leaving the little toddler out, she spoke to Ivy, who by now had let go of her mother's legs and had come over to stand next to Holly.

Would Holly really be happy with just nieces and nephews in her life? Didn't most women want kids? She looked like a natural. Soft and nurturing and compassionate—all the qualities he had longed for in his mother but had found sadly lacking.

It suddenly occurred to him that as an only child he would never have nieces or nephews.

But he was fine about it. Of course he was. He'd seen the way kids suffered during a bitter divorce. Even the amicable ones were still disruptive to a child. He didn't want the ties and commitment of a wife and children. Call him a cynic, but how soon would this harried young mother get tired of the drudgery of motherhood? Or the overworked husband, tired of coming home to a wife who was now only interested in sleeping, not sex. He knew some people made a decent go of it and he admired them for it.

But it wasn't for him.

CHAPTER NINE

HOLLY HANDED THE darling little baby—who adorable Ivy had proudly informed her was called Felix—back to his mother and soon after the young family left the café. She had been conscious of Zack watching her with the children, but she hadn't been able to disguise the delight she'd experienced in interacting with them. Delight and an acute feeling of despair. She had told herself marriage and kids were no longer her mission in life, but holding that gorgeous baby boy made her realise how much she wanted children. She wanted the whole family package—love and commitment from a man who would stand by her and help her raise a family.

Didn't most people long for that?

Zack would be a wonderful family man but he claimed he didn't want to go down that path. But she couldn't imagine going down it with anyone else. How could she think of a future with someone else when the only man she wanted was him? The intimacy they'd shared had shown her what she'd missed out on before, but it wasn't just about amazing sex. It was the way he treated her, the way he cared for her, the way he spoke to her and the way he listened to her. All the things that made a great relationship.

Zack drained his coffee cup and placed it back on its saucer. 'I should've given her a business card.'

Holly stiffened. 'Why?'

His mouth was tilted in a cynical smile. 'How long do you reckon before she'll get sick of it all? Or her husband gets sick of her and the kids and the domestic chaos?'

She pressed her lips together, annoyed he was reminding her of how little he wanted what she wanted. What she'd denied she wanted. 'That's a horrible thing to say. She looked happy enough, a little tired and hassled, but that's to be expected when you've got small children.'

'The odds are stacked against her. Forty-nine per cent of marriages end up in divorce.'

'But she might be in the fifty-one per cent who make it,' Holly said. 'Like my parents. They're as in love today as they were the day they met.'

His lips made a shrugging movement and he lifted one hip to take his wallet out of his back pocket to pay for their coffees. 'You looked pretty comfortable with those kids.'

Holly couldn't meet his gaze and looked at the

paper sugar sachets in a jar on the table instead. 'I love kids. It doesn't mean I want them for myself.'

There was a silence. A you're-not-telling-the-truth silence.

She looked up to see him looking at her with a frown. 'What's the matter?'

He gave a brief lopsided smile but it didn't involve his eyes. 'Come on.' He scraped back his chair and stood. 'We have some sightseeing to do.'

The rest of the day was as magical as any warm spring day in Paris could be. Zack took her to the Eiffel Tower and they stood together and gazed at the spectacular view of Paris below. After a late lunch, they walked back along the Seine and wandered in and out of shops and boutiques. At one stage he let her wander on her own for a bit as he said he had a couple of calls to make. They met back up half an hour later and she told him about a gorgeous butter-soft dove-grey leather jacket she'd seen in an up-market boutique and he'd insisted on her showing him and then promptly bought it for her.

Finally, they made their way back to their hotel to get ready for the night out Zack had planned.

Holly had a quick shower and was dressed in nothing but a towel and was doing her hair and make-up in the hotel suite's luxurious bathroom when Zack came in. He too was in the process of getting ready and was only wearing his underwear. He slipped his arms around her from behind and a wave of longing swept through her at the intimate contact of his pelvis against the cheeks of her bottom. She leaned her head to one side as his mouth went to her neck and she shivered all over when his tongue flicked against her earlobe.

'You smell beautiful.' His husky voice was as sexy as his caress and the temptation of his body pressing her from behind sent her senses spinning.

She turned in his arms, winding her arms around his neck, and gave him a teasing smile. 'You're not bored with me yet?'

He brushed her lips with his. 'Not yet. You?'

Never. Holly pressed herself closer, her body aching for his possession. 'Not yet.'

'Good.' He kissed her again, a leisurely kiss that was both tender and passionate, his tongue mating with hers in a slow dance that made her blood race and her legs weaken. He gathered her closer, the hard ridge of his erection stirring her body into a fevered response. He tugged away her towel and tossed it aside. She removed his underwear and they came back together, skin on skin.

He lifted her in his arms and carried her to the bedroom, laying her down on the bed and coming down beside her. He kissed his way from her mouth to her breasts, leaving a trail of fire in his wake. Her skin tingled and tightened with the torturous pleasure of his touch. Need spiralled through her, a tight aching need that begged to be assuaged. He took his time caressing her breasts, suckling on her nipples, teasing the pink areoles and then taking his mouth lower to the swollen heart of her body.

It was a slow and deliberate torture. He kept her hanging on the edge of bliss, pulling back time and time again until she was begging, sobbing, pleading shamelessly for release. 'Now. Now. Now.'

He moved back over her and entered her in a deep thrust that made her gasp in delight. *At last. At last. At last.* But, unlike the other times he'd made love to her, he took his time, his movements within her body slow, deliberately, torturously slow, until she was clawing at his back and shoulders, digging her hands into his buttocks, urging him on like a sex-crazed addict.

He brought his mouth back to hers in a drugging kiss that made the roots of her hair lift away from her scalp. He kept thrusting, deeply but slowly, ramping up her need to a level she hadn't experienced before. She would die if he didn't make her come. She would chain him to the bed and have her wicked way with him. For weeks. Months. Years.

For ever.

Holly stiffened. No. Not for ever. He didn't want for ever.

Zack stilled his movements and frowned. 'Did I hurt you?'

She let out a shaky breath. 'No. But I'm going to kill you if you don't make me come.'

His smile made something in her belly swoop. 'You're always in such a rush, sweetheart. Slow is much better.'

Holly fisted her hands in his hair. 'I want you. I'm going crazy here.'

He began thrusting again, gradually building up his pace, each movement stoking the fire of her need. She moved with him, urging him with each upward movement of her body, aching for the moment when she would fly free.

And then finally, *finally* he slipped a hand between their sweat-slicked bodies and took her over the edge. She was swept up into an earth-shattering orgasm, the spasms rippling through her in pulsating waves. Just when she thought it was over, he would caress her again and the pleasure would return more intensely, each ripple and spasm making her cry out in ecstasy. She thought she was going to lose consciousness. Surely it wasn't possible to feel such mind-blowing pleasure? It took over her entire body, her limbs, her torso, her inner core alive with sensation. Tingling, tantalising sensations that made her wonder if she would survive such a sensual onslaught.

Zack continued thrusting, building to his own release, and Holly held him as he tensed and then shuddered through it, each pumping action sending another wave of sensation through her flesh. He collapsed over her, his breathing laboured, his essence warm and damp between her legs.

Holly lay with him for long silent minutes, thinking about that baby back in the café. If she and Zack were in a committed and long-term relationship, making a baby together would be the perfectly normal thing to do. She pictured their baby, a tiny boy with dark hair and sapphire-blue eyes or maybe a little girl with chestnut hair... Okay, okay, *red hair* and pale skin and brown eyes.

But how could she have a baby with a man who didn't want to be with her for ever? A man who didn't believe in the fairy tale, who was so cynical about relationships he actively avoided being with someone longer than a month or six weeks at most?

How could she settle for a temporary 'engagement' with him when she wanted more? So much more. She wanted what her parents had. She wanted what her sisters had. She wanted love that lasted. Love that would ride out the tough and the tender, the happy times and the sad. She wanted her dream wedding, stating those sacred vows to the man she loved, and hearing him say them to her, making promises she had longed to hear all of her life. The promise to love and protect and to worship her with his body.

Zack had offered her his body but it was all he was prepared to give her. She wanted more—she wanted a man who would willingly and unreservedly open his heart to her. Zack wasn't that man, so why was she wasting time wishing and hoping he was? He had made it clear what he wanted out of their relationship. And it wasn't enough for her. Not now that she had come to her senses and realised what she wanted more than anything else.

Zack shifted his weight, rolling onto his side, and looked at her with a glinting smile. 'What did I tell you? Slow is much better.'

Holly gave him a fleeting smile that was little more than a twitch of her lips. 'You're very good at this stuff.' *At making me perilously close to falling in love with you.*

His smile faded and a small frown appeared between his eyebrows. He drew in a breath and brushed her hair back from her forehead. 'Is everything okay, sweetheart?'

Sweetheart. Oh, how she wished she truly were his sweetheart. His soul mate. The person he had opened his heart to. But they were just empty words he used—they didn't mean anything. How could they when his heart was securely locked away?

Holly pushed away from him and got off the bed and picked up her discarded towel and wrapped it sarong-like around her body. She couldn't think straight with him holding her. Tempting her.

No. It was crunch time. It was time to be honest about her feelings. She couldn't continue any other

way. It wasn't honest. It wasn't fair. It wasn't digni-
fied to go on pretending.

'Holly, darling—what's wrong?' He got off the
bed in one movement and came to her, his hands
on her upper arms, his touch gentle, concern etched
on his face.

Holly squeezed back the sting of tears at his use
of the word *darling*. She didn't want to do the weepy
lover thing. She had too much pride. 'You call me
such wonderful endearments. Sweetheart, darling,
sweetie, but they're just words to you. They don't
mean anything, do they?'

His frown carved deeper into his forehead. 'What
are you talking about? We're in an intimate relationship. What's wrong with me using endearments?'

'We're in a relationship with a clock ticking,
that's why,' Holly said. 'That's not what I'd call intimate. You don't want what I want. What I've always wanted.'

His hands fell away from her arms and he picked
up his towel and wrapped it around his hips. His
movements were slow, measured and unnaturally
calm as if he was controlling his reaction. His emotions. 'You told me you didn't want the fairy tale.'
His voice had the same measured calm of his movements. Almost too calm. Too controlled.

Holly could feel him retreating from her and a
hollow space opened in her stomach, all her hopes
and dreams sucking into the abyss of despair like

sand sliding into a sinkhole. 'I know I did. But I was lying to you and to myself.' She took a breath for courage and continued, 'I know you said we were to keep our emotions out of this but I can't promise that any more.'

A guarded look came into his eyes like a drawbridge slowing raised up on a fortress. 'What are you saying?'

Holly swallowed the sudden lump in her throat. 'I'm not saying I'm in love with you, but I can't go on with this fling between us because it wouldn't be right. For me, I mean. I don't want to get too involved with a man who isn't capable of giving me what I want.'

His jaw worked as if he was biting down on his back molars. His eyes shifted away from hers, his hand pushing through his hair as if it was irritating him. 'I'm sorry, sweet—I mean, Holly.' His voice had a raw edge to it. 'You're saying you're not in love and yet you want to end it? That doesn't make sense.'

'It makes sense to me,' Holly said. 'I've been down this road twice before and I don't want to go down it again. I don't want to get hurt. You have the potential to hurt me if I fall in love with you.'

'Then don't fall in love with me. Simple.' He gave a mirthless laugh as if even he wasn't entirely convinced his suggestion would work.

'Zack, listen to me.' Holly held his gaze. 'You've

always insisted you don't want marriage and kids. I've realised I *do* want those things. I want them so much it hurts. Holding that baby earlier today was like torture. I can't bear the thought of never having my own family. I've been raised in a loving family and I want to do the same for my kids if I'm so lucky to have them.'

'Look, you can have a family in a year or two with someone else, surely? What's the rush? You're still young and—'

'I'm not prepared to waste any more time with going-nowhere relationships.' Holly turned away to compose herself. The longer she looked at him the harder it was to stay strong. 'I know this is hard, me springing this on you like this, but I would feel like I was compromising everything I hold dear by stay-ing with you this week. I can't be in a fling when I want for ever. I don't want to get hurt, and you, Zack, have the potential to hurt me more than anyone has done in the past.'

His hands came down on her shoulders and he turned her to face him. 'It was never my intention to hurt you.' His dark blue gaze was worried, bleak, tortured as if the thought of inflicting pain on her was anathema to him. 'You're a wonderful person. An amazing person, but I told you from the start—'

'Please don't say it,' Holly said, her heart contract-ing, squeezing the last trace of hope out of her chest like the last bit of toothpaste out of a tube. 'I've had this speech twice already from both of my exes. The it's-not-you-it's-me speech.'

He dropped his hands from her shoulders and stepped back, using one hand to rake through his hair again. He let out a curse word not quite under his breath. He swung his gaze back to hers, his eyes accusing—wounded but on attack. 'Why are you bringing this up now?'

Holly turned away to pull on some clothes, her movements jerky and uncoordinated as she desperately tried to keep control of her spiralling emotions. 'I told you why. Because I would be hurting myself more by not speaking up.'

There was a brittle silence. The atmosphere so tight it felt like it would explode.

Holly set to pulling on her clothes before she changed her mind. Standing half-naked anywhere near Zack was too much for her self-control. She had to stay resolute. She had to get out while her heart was still in one piece.

'What are you doing?' There was a sharp note in his voice.

'I'm getting dressed.'

'But you're wearing casual clothes. I've booked dinner and a show and dancing after that.'

Holly turned from zipping up her jeans to look at him. 'I'm going home. Tonight. I think it's for the best.'

'You *think*?' He almost spat the word at her, his

eyes blazing. 'No wonder your business has taken a hit if you treat an expensive trip to Paris as if it's nothing.'

Holly mentally counted to ten. She didn't want to turn this into a slanging match. 'I'll reimburse you for the money you've spent.' Her stomach churned at the thought of how much she would have to repay him. First-class airfares. A penthouse suite in a luxury hotel. All those wonderful flowers—she of all people knew how much they would have cost. The designer leather jacket. The engagement ring... She looked at it glinting on her finger, as if to say, *I told you so*. She hadn't listened to the bell of warning, but she was listening now. She slid the ring off her finger and handed it to him. 'I can't keep this. It wouldn't be right.'

He ignored the ring sitting in the middle of her palm. 'What about your sister's engagement party?'

She let out a long sigh. 'I'll go alone. It's what I should've realised well before now. I shouldn't feel ashamed in front of my family for not being able to find a man who will love me and commit to me. If it happens it happens. All I can do is be a good person, stay true to my values and hope one day it pays off.' She pushed the ring towards him again. 'Please take it back.'

He pushed her hand away. 'Keep it. Sell it. Throw it out of the window for all I care.'

Holly was tempted to do exactly that. She pictured herself walking over to the window overlooking the

Jardin des Tuileries and tossing the ring to the ground below. Then she would throw out all the flowers he'd bought her, bunch by bunch, vase by vase, watching them scatter and shatter like her dreams. But instead she left the ring on the bedside table on his side of the bed. 'I'm sorry, Zack. I know you're upset, but—'

'Upset?' He gave a savage-sounding laugh. 'I'm not upset. Do you think you have the power to hurt me?'

Holly reared back as if he'd slapped her. But then she took a deep calming breath, keeping her voice steady even though it cost her dearly. 'No one has the power to hurt you. You won't allow them to. That's why you live your life the way you do. From shallow relationship to shallow relationship. A week here. A week there. A one-night stand or two and on you move.'

'I'm fine with my life,' he said in the same harsh tone that slashed at her like flick knives. 'It was perfectly fine until I met you.'

'And why is that? Because I made you feel something you don't normally feel?' Holly knew she was pushing him but she didn't want to leave him unless she was absolutely sure he didn't care for her. If he didn't, at the very least, show some *potential* to love her.

Every muscle on his face tensed as if turned to marble. Frozen impenetrable marble. His eyes became shuttered, a screen rolling down until all she could see was his disdain showing through the slats. 'I'll call a cab for you.'

Her heart plummeted, torn from its moorings like a yacht in a vicious storm. She couldn't breathe. Was she having a panic attack? Or was her heart breaking into a thousand pieces? 'That would be great. Thank you.' How had she managed to sound so calm? So damned *polite*?

Holly gathered the rest of her things, packing like an automaton, conscious of Zack watching her with an inscrutable expression on his face. She dawdled over folding her clothes into her bag, hoping he would have a change of mind—a change of heart.

But did he even have a heart?

Finally it was done. She was packed and ready to leave. Not ready, really. Holly would have given anything to be spending the rest of the week with him. But she couldn't do so without losing a part of herself. A part of herself that was finally brave and honest enough to openly express what she wanted.

What she longed for with all her heart.

Zack followed her to the door of the suite, even carrying her bag for her as if he was one of the hotel's valets and not the man who had made passionate love to her only minutes before. He was wearing a bathrobe now—he had switched it for the towel as if he needed a thicker barrier. But wasn't that the whole problem? He had barriers up. Cast-iron emotional barriers that allowed no one to get through.

Holly stood at the door of the suite and held out her hand but he ignored it in the same way he'd ignored her return of his engagement ring. She sighed and dropped her hand back by her side. 'I'm sorry it has to end this way. But if I were to fall in love with you, then things would be even more—'

'You're not one bit sorry.' His embittered gaze cut her to the quick. 'You say you're worried about falling in love with me. What sort of crazy excuse is that? You planned this from the start, didn't you? This was your mission to get back at all the men who'd disappointed you. Your attempt to turn the tables like they'd been turned on you. The only difference being I don't care.'

Holly had never wanted to slap someone more than at that moment. She wanted to slap him and punch him and tear his hair out by the roots. She wanted to thump him against the heart so he could feel the pain he'd inflicted on hers. It terrified her how angry she was. It shocked her. Shamed her. Shattered her. No one had hurt her more than he had at that moment. Her two cancelled weddings were nothing compared to this.

She sucked in a breath and let it out in a self-calming stream. 'This is not about revenge. It's about me finally being honest with myself. I can't let myself fall in love with a man who won't love me back.'

He opened the door as if he couldn't wait for her

to leave. 'Have a nice flight.' His sarcasm was the final dagger stab through her heart.

Holly picked up her bag and her dashed hopes and left.

CHAPTER TEN

Zack closed the door on just short of a slam. He wanted to slam that door till it splintered. He wanted to punch a hole through it with his fist. He wanted to thump and thump and thump it until his hand was a bleeding pulp.

He wanted. He wanted. He wanted.

Anger rose in him like a red mist, blinding his eyes, barrelling through his chest like a runaway train. He hadn't seen it coming. What sort of fool had he turned into? Holly had ripped the rug from under him just like his mother had done to him and his father. Blindsided him. *Hurt him.* And just like twenty-four years ago when his mother had left him and his father, he had been torn with the need to run to her, to beg, to plead with her to stay.

But he hadn't.

Of course he hadn't, because he didn't allow himself to feel that deeply about anyone. Not even a cute little redhead with pearly skin and a smile that lit up a room. Not even when she rocked him to the core with her sensuality. Not even when she made him, for the first time in his life, think of babies and time that stretched on for ever. Not even when she made him think that maybe, maybe they would be different. The one couple who could make it.

But no. *No. No. No. No. No.* How many times did he have to say it? He didn't allow himself to think along those lines.

He had seen too much. Felt too much. *Hurt* too damn much to want any of it. He was glad Holly had left. He had been a fool to bring her to Paris. Paris? The City of Love? What a joke. It was the city of disappointment.

The city of bitter, gut-shredding disappointment.

He paced the room, part of him splitting off in his mind and running after her, just like he had run after his mother all those years ago. He had clung to her, pleaded, begged her to stay to keep their family intact. But his mother had shaken him off as if he were a piece of lint clinging to her designer outfit. Nothing he had said or done had been able to change her mind and so he had stopped begging and pleading. He had made a promise to his ten-year-old self that he would never beg. Never plead.

Never love.

Zack drew in a breath but his chest felt tight. Tight and painful like he was having an asthma attack. But it wasn't asthma—it was reality coming home to roost. The reality that if you gave people the potential to hurt you, that was exactly what they did. Time and time again. Like clockwork. Didn't he see it every day at work? The walking wounded came into his office and begged him to fix things for them.

But he was no magician. He couldn't restore people's feelings to make them what they had once been. People got together and then they parted. Some parted with bitterness, some parted with politeness. He was fine with that. He made a living out of that— a decent living, a living other people envied.

Then why did he feel a strange sense of disquiet... as if his life was lacking something?

Holly wasn't in love with him but was apparently worried she might do so. What sort of crazy excuse was that? It was taking self-protection to a whole new level.

Like you can talk.

Zack clenched his jaw until his molars threatened mutiny. Okay, so his conscience had made a good point, but he wasn't interested in falling in love. He didn't have the falling in love gene. He had too much pride to go after Holly. What would be the point? He didn't want to fall in love with her either.

He'd been a fool to think she'd be satisfied with a temporary fling. She had fairy tale written all over her. He wasn't after the fairy tale. The princes and princesses of the fairy tale ended up in his office, paying him to represent them in dirty divorces. And he had enjoyed the dirty ones the most. Relished the role of getting justice for those who had been hard done by in a relationship.

It was his tagline, for God's sake—*Get Zack Knight and Get Even.*

But why, standing in this empty hotel room, did he feel as if something essential to him, something he couldn't function without had walked out of that door with Holly?

Holly caught the first flight she could back to London, wincing at the amount of money she was spending on a short-notice flight. But she had to get away. She couldn't waste any more time wishing and hoping Zack would change his mind and come after her. She'd made a gamble in expressing her feelings but it had failed. Miserably, painfully failed.

If he cared anything for her, wouldn't he have come after her? But no. He didn't want to spend for ever with her. He used terms of endearment but he didn't mean them. Had never meant them. Not like her parents meant them. Affectionate and tender terms that signalled a long-term commitment to the other's happiness.

Hadn't she spent her entire life witnessing it and wanting it for herself?

Holly looked down at her empty ring finger. How stupid had she been to think that ring had represented something? How naïve to think he had actually *cared* about her. He didn't care. He was incapable of it. He had locked away his heart, surrounded it with an impenetrable fortress.

Why, oh, why had she chosen yet another man who didn't have the capacity, the *willingness* to love her?

Holly was back at work on Monday morning, making an arrangement for a mother with a newborn baby, another one of her previous wedding clients who was experiencing the fairy tale that had so far eluded her. She looked up from her handiwork when Sabrina came in carrying coffees on a cardboard tray.

Sabrina didn't have her usual bright chirpiness about her, but who was *she* to talk?

'Okay, so what happened? How come you didn't stay the whole week in Paris?' Sabrina asked, making Holly regret texting her as she'd boarded the plane last night. She needed more time to think, to reflect over how things had panned out.

She needed more time to *heal*.

'It started well and ended badly. But I'd rather not talk about it.'

Sabrina frowned and handed Holly a flat white with two sugars. 'Good. Then I won't tell you about my disastrous weekend either.'

Holly took a sip, welcoming the much-needed caffeine. 'Let me guess. You ran into Max Firbank at a family function.'

Sabrina's cheeks flared with vivid colour. 'You wouldn't believe me if I told you what happened between me and Max on Saturday night.'

'Try me.'

Sabrina perched on one of the workbench stools and sighed. 'I don't know what came over me. Seriously, I need therapy or something. We were at a mutual friend's dinner party. Why I agreed to go, I have no idea. I didn't bring my car as it was in the workshop being serviced—I didn't get back in time on Friday to pick it up. Max offered to drive me home and then...' Her blush deepened and she continued, 'We kind of...kissed.'

Holly nearly spilt her coffee. 'Seriously?'

Sabrina screwed up her face. 'I know. I know. I know. It was a stupid thing to do, but we'd been arguing on the way home, you know, like we nearly always do. We arrived at my flat and he walked me to the door and then we were inside and alone with the door closed. I was mid-sentence and suddenly he took me by the arms, pulled me towards him. I thought he was about to kiss me but then he seemed to stop himself. So then I kind of moved my mouth closer to his...'

'And?'

Sabrina's tongue touched her lips as if she were recalling that stolen kiss. 'It was just a kiss. Nothing else. It was over almost as soon as it began, as if he despised himself for kissing me. And then he left.'

'Did you...enjoy it?'

Sabrina gave a crack of laughter but it didn't sound convincing. 'Why would I? I hate him. Always have, always will. But enough about me. Tell me what happened in Paris?'

Holly let out a jagged sigh. 'I came back early.'

'But why?'

Holly ran her finger around the cardboard rim of her cup. 'I couldn't maintain the pretence any longer. I told him I was worried about falling in love with him. He didn't take it too well.'

Sabrina frowned. 'But you are in love with him, right? I mean, it's pretty obvious to me you are.'

Holly looked at her friend with the intention of denying it, but then she realised it would be pointless. She did love Zack. She had loved him from the first kiss. Wasn't that why she had agreed to their 'engagement'? Wasn't that why she'd gone with him to Paris? She loved him with all her heart. The heart she had never opened to anyone quite like that before. Her previous relationships were a cheap imitation, but her love for Zack was the real deal. Real and lasting and oh, so terribly painful.

'Yes, I am in love with him. But he hasn't got the capacity to love. He would never allow himself to be that vulnerable.'

Sabrina's expression folded in empathy. 'Oh, Holly, I'm so sorry. But you've only been dating such a short time. Maybe he needs a little more time.'

'I can't spend another minute of my life hoping a man will fall in love with me,' Holly said. 'Zack's had barriers up from the start. He won't fall in love with me because he won't allow himself to. I can't be with a man who only gives me his body.'

'It's one heck of a body.' Sabrina's mouth twisted. 'Almost as hot as Max's. But I did wonder if things would turn out like this. Zack's not the settling down type.' She blew out a sigh. 'Just like Max.'

Holly stared at her friend. 'Are you sure you hate Max as much as you make out?'

Sabrina couldn't have looked more sheepish if she had her hand stuck in a double chocolate-chip cookie jar. 'It was a pretty awesome kiss.'

Holly knew all about pretty awesome kisses. They made you fall in love. Hard. 'Are you going to see him again?'

Sabrina gave a tight-lipped smile. 'Not if I can help it.'

CHAPTER ELEVEN

ZACK STUBBORNLY REFUSED to fly back from Paris until he was good and ready. He'd paid good money for the hotel and the conference and he wasn't going to waste it. But there was no city worse for being on your own than Paris. It wasn't called the City of Love for nothing. Everywhere he looked there were couples walking hand in hand or arm in arm. He even walked past a wedding party on Wednesday in the Jardins des Tuileries and he felt sick to his stomach. Who was so desperate to get married on a weekday? *There goes another couple of silly fools.* He spoke the words in his head but strangely, instead of feeling his normal cynical amusement, he felt…sad.

Deeply, miserably sad.

Was this how his father had felt after Zack's mother left him? Like the colour had been taken out of his days? Was this ache in the region of his heart, this tugging, tearing, torturous ache, what his father had felt for the last twenty-four years? No wonder his dad had barely functioned. Zack was barely functioning himself. He was a zombie walking through the streets of Paris, one foot moving in front of the other like a robot with a rundown battery.

He had to get a grip on himself. He wasn't that ten-year-old kid any more who cried himself to sleep because he wanted his family to stay together. People came and went in his life all the time and he was fine about it. Perfectly fine. Holly had made her choice and he would be fine with it too.

Eventually.

But shouldn't he make an announcement that their 'engagement' was over? For some strange reason, he felt reluctant to do so. Not just because of the way the press would carry on, but because he needed time to think. It was still too new, too raw, which was weird because he'd never felt raw after a break-up before. Relief was what he normally felt. He'd seen what a bad break-up could do to a man. He'd been picking up the pieces of his father for decades. Zack had somewhat ruthlessly avoided any involvement with a woman who had the potential to devastate him.

Why, then, was he feeling so damn devastated?

Holly was expecting the news about her third broken 'engagement' to go viral on social media but, strangely, nothing was reported. Was Zack intent on keeping the charade going? But why? He hadn't even contacted her. Not even a text message. She didn't want to be the one to report their break-up, even though she had called her parents and told them everything. It had been strangely cathartic to do so. Her mother and father had been their usual wonderfully supportive selves, reassuring her that one day she would find true love.

If only Holly could believe it.

The good news was her business was still on the rise. Wedding bookings were being made just about every day. Whatever negative energy had been around before had gone. But it was a special type of torture sitting down with a bride-to-be and helping her choose bouquet designs for her wedding. A heart-wrenching torture because Holly wished she were planning *her* wedding.

Her dream wedding to the only man she could ever love.

Zack dragged himself to attend a dinner his dad had organised in order for him to meet his new partner, Kayla. He'd told his dad Holly couldn't make it but he hadn't gone into any details. He wasn't ready to cross that treacherous bridge just yet.

He sat through a delicious home-cooked meal Kayla had prepared but he might as well have been eating sawdust. Watching his dad and Kayla interact was a painful reminder of how much he missed

Holly. Hadn't *he* looked at Holly like his dad was looking at Kayla? He still hadn't contacted her since he'd come back from Paris. He kept picking up his phone, his fingers hovering over the screen, but then he would draw a blank. What could he say? *Come back to me?*

No way would he ever text something like that. He didn't have a begging bone in his body. He was the one who said when a relationship was over. So Holly had got the better of him? He could deal with it. He'd dealt with rejection before. His mother had left him as well as his father and he'd handled that, hadn't he? Handled it so well he had never been rejected again...

Until now.

Zack closed his eyes on a tight blink, but even behind his eyelids he could see her. Holly. Gorgeous, sensuous Holly with a smile that could melt steel and a body that could send his hormones into a seizure.

'Is everything all right?' Kayla glanced at his barely touched meal. 'You're not eating.'

Zack picked up his knife and fork and forced a smile. 'Sorry. I'm not all that hungry.'

His dad exchanged a knowing look with Kayla. 'He's lovesick, that's why.' He picked up the freshly baked bread rolls that were in a basket and handed it to Zack. 'It's a shame Holly couldn't make it tonight. We're dying to meet her, aren't we, darling?'

'Absolutely,' Kayla said, smiling. 'She did the flowers for my niece's wedding. They were amazing.'

'Yes…she's pretty amazing.' Zack took the roll but he knew it wouldn't get past the lump in his throat. Of course Holly was amazing. Everything about her was amazing. She'd ended their fling because she hadn't wanted to fall in love with him. Newsflash. *He* was in love with her. Desperately in love. Ridiculously and against all odds in love because no one had rocked his world like her. No one ever would because Holly held the key to his locked-away heart. Her feistiness, her fighting spirit, her phenomenal sensuality had kicked away the barricade around his heart like someone kicking away soggy cardboard.

How could he not have realised until now he had feelings for her? Feelings that had been there from the moment he'd met her. The connection he'd felt had been on a cellular level. The feelings had frightened him so much he had disguised them, hidden them, suppressed them. Denied them. But they were refusing to be ignored. They were clamouring inside him, ballooning in his chest until he could scarcely take a breath.

'Are you okay?' Kayla leaned forward in concern.

Zack pushed back his chair and tossed his napkin to the side. 'I'm fine. I'm great.' He gave a laugh, a shocked-sounding laugh because he'd been so blind about how he felt. 'I'm in love.'

Kayla and his dad exchanged another look and reached for each other's hands.

'But of course you are,' his dad said with a wide smile. 'Welcome to the club.'

Holly was spending a quiet night at the flat, sketching some bouquet designs for a wedding next month. There was a knock on the door and she groaned. Why couldn't Mrs Fry ask for a cup of sugar like normal people? Three days in a row her landlady had knocked at her door to report some supposed misdemeanour of one of the neighbours. Holly suspected her landlady's visits had more to do with Mrs Fry's desire to find out why Zack hadn't been around since he'd picked her up for the Paris trip. She'd noticed Mrs Fry glancing at her bare ring finger a few times but, unusually for her, hadn't said anything.

Holly rose from the sofa, went to answer the door and her heart leapt when she saw Zack standing there holding a huge bunch of red roses.

'Hi...' she said.

'Can I come in?' His voice had an odd note of uncertainty as if he wasn't sure of his welcome.

'Sure.' She opened the door wider and he came in, bringing the scent of roses and cool night air with him. She closed the door and directed him to take a seat on the sofa but he shook his head and came closer, holding the roses out to her.

'For you.'

'They're gorgeous, thank you…' Holly took the bouquet and breathed in the heady fragrance of the roses.

With an impatient sound, Zack grabbed the roses off her and put them to one side and took her by the hands. 'We'll get to the flowers later. I have something important to get off my chest. I've been a fool, my darling. A stupid, stubborn fool, who was too blind, too frightened, too cowardly to recognise the feelings I have for you. I love you. Can you forgive me for not telling you sooner?'

Holly was so shocked, so pleasantly, blissfully shocked she stood frozen, not sure she trusted what she'd heard. 'You…you love me?'

His eyes were so soft and warm it brought tears to hers. 'So, so much. I think I fell in love with you at Kendra's divorce party.' His voice choked over the words and she knew then it was true. He loved her. He really loved her.

Holly threw herself into his arms and he picked her up and turned her in a circle, his face wreathed in smiles. 'I love you so much,' she said, gazing into his suspiciously moist gaze. 'I love, love, love you.'

He pressed a series of kisses all over her face, hugging her so tightly she could barely breathe. Then he set her back on her feet and kept his arms around her as if he never wanted to let her go. 'Please do me the honour of becoming my wife. I want to spend for ever with you. I want the fairy tale—*our* fairy tale, because I know with every fibre of my being that no one could ever complete me, excite me and fulfil me like you do.'

Holly had never heard a more heartfelt and earnest proposal, and she should know as she'd received two others. Well, one if she was honest, as she had issued the first proposal. The sincerity in Zack's tone, the desperate appeal in his gaze as if he was worried that even at this point she might still reject him confirmed how deeply he cared about her. No one could ever make her feel so loved, so treasured, so adored as Zack. He was openly tearing up, his voice choking and his expression so full of love, it made her heart swell like it was taking over every space inside her chest.

'Of course I'll marry you,' she said, smiling and crying at the same time. 'I adore you. I want to spend the rest of my life loving you.'

He brushed at his eyes with his sleeve. 'I don't deserve you after what I did to you in Paris. Letting you leave like that. Speaking to you like that. What was I thinking? I should've come after you. I was so angry and so stubborn I ended up staying the whole week, and I can safely say I have never felt so damn miserable.'

Holly stroked his lean jaw. 'Poor darling. I was pretty miserable too. I'm sorry I walked out on you like that, but I really felt I had to be honest with you.

Not that I was being honest in telling you I wasn't in love with you. But I didn't want to admit how I felt about you to myself, let alone you.'

Zack cupped her face in his hands. 'When I saw you holding that baby in the café…for the first time in my life I thought about the possibility of having a family. It took me a few days to realise how much I want to be a father.'

'You want a family?'

He smiled and held her hand against his heart. 'The only person I could ever think of raising a family with is you. That's why it's never been an option for me until now. I know you will be a wonderful mother. An amazing mother because everything about you is amazing.'

Holly wondered if it were possible to be any happier. She looped her arms around his neck and pressed a kiss to his lips. 'I can't wait to have your babies. Nothing would bring me more joy than sharing that experience with you.'

He stroked the hair away from her forehead, his expression so tender it made her throat thicken. 'We'll be good at this, my darling.' His voice was husky, raw with emotion. 'At marriage, at commitment, at loving each other for ever. I promise you I'll always be there for you no matter what. Your happiness is my happiness.'

Holly smiled and reached up to kiss him again.

'I don't think I could ever be happier than I am in this moment.'

'Oh, you'll be happier,' he said, bringing his mouth down to hers. 'I'm going to make sure of it.'

* * * * *

If you enjoyed
Claimed for the Billionaire's Convenience,
you're sure to enjoy these other
Melanie Milburne stories!

The Tycoon's Marriage Deal
A Ring for the Greek's Baby
Blackmailed into the Marriage Bed
Bound by a One-Night Vow

Available now!

#3693 A DEAL FOR THE SICILIAN'S DIAMOND
Conveniently Wed!
by Michelle Smart
Aislin will do anything to secure money for her sick nephew—even pose as billionaire Dante's fiancée at a society wedding. Yet soon their explosive passion rips through the terms of their arrangement, leaving them both hungry for more...

#3694 THE PRINCE'S RUTHLESS WEDDING VOW
by Jane Porter
When Josephine rescues a drowning stranger, she's captivated. Until it's revealed that he's Prince Alexander, heir to the throne of Aargau... Now the threat of scandal means this shy Cinderella must become a royal bride!

#3695 INNOCENT QUEEN BY ROYAL COMMAND
Claimed by a King
by Kelly Hunter
King Augustus is shocked when his country delivers him a courtesan. But Sera's surprising innocence and undisguised yearning for him pushes Augustus's self-control to the limits. Now he won't rest until Sera becomes his queen!

#3696 BILLIONAIRE'S PRISONER IN PARADISE
by Annie West
Finding herself incognito and captive on Alexei's private island, Princess Mina must convince him *she's* his future bride. But after a night in the Greek's bed, there's more at stake than her hidden identity—her heart is at Alexei's mercy, too!

YOU CAN FIND MORE INFORMATION ON UPCOMING HARLEQUIN® TITLES, FREE EXCERPTS AND MORE AT WWW.HARLEQUIN.COM.

HPCNM0119RB

Get 4 FREE REWARDS!

We'll send you 2 FREE Books plus 2 FREE Mystery Gifts.

Harlequin Presents® books feature a sensational and sophisticated world of international romance where sinfully tempting heroes ignite passion.

FREE Value Over $20

*Aislin will do anything to secure money for her sick
nephew—even pose as billionaire Dante's fiancée at a
society wedding. Yet soon their explosive passion rips
through the terms of their arrangement, leaving them
both hungry for more…*

*Read on for a sneak preview of
Michelle Smart's next story,*
The Sicilian's Bought Cinderella.

"But…" Aislin couldn't form anything more than that one syllable.
Dante's offer had thrown her completely.

His smile was rueful. "My offer is simple, *dolcezza.* You come
to the wedding with me and I give you a million euros."

He pronounced it *"seemple,"* a quirk she would have found
endearing if her brain hadn't frozen into a stunned snowball.

"You want to pay me to come to a wedding with you?"

"Si." He unfolded his arms and spread his hands. "The money
will be yours. You can give as much or as little of it to your sister."

It took a huge amount of effort to keep her voice steady. "But
you must have a heap of women you could take and not have to
pay them for it."

"None of them are suitable."

"What does that mean?"

"I need to make an impression on someone and having you on
my arm will assist in that."

"A million dollars for one afternoon?"

"I never said it would be for an afternoon. The celebrations will
take place over the coming weekend."

She tugged at her ponytail. "Weekend?"

"Aislin, the groom is one of Sicily's richest men. It is a necessity that his wedding be the biggest and flashiest it can be."

She almost laughed at the deadpan way he explained it.

She didn't need to ask who the richest man in Sicily was.

"If I'm going to accept your offer, what else do I need to know?"

"Nothing… Apart from that I will be introducing you as my fiancée."

"What?" Aislin winced at the squeakiness of her tone.

"I require you to play the role of my fiancée." His grin was wide with just a touch of ruefulness. The deadened, shocked look that had rung from his eyes only a few minutes before had gone. Now they sparkled with life, and it was almost hypnotizing.

She blinked the effect away.

"Why do you need a fiancée?"

"Because the father of the bride thinks going into business with me will damage his reputation."

"How?"

"I will go through the reasons once I have your agreement on the matter. I appreciate it is a lot to take in so I'm going to leave you to sleep on it. You can give me your answer in the morning. If you're in agreement then I shall take you home with me and give you more details. We will have a few days to get to know each other and work on putting on a convincing act."

"And if I say no?"

He shrugged. "If you say no, then no million euros."

Don't miss
The Sicilian's Bought Cinderella,
available February 2019 wherever
Harlequin Presents® books and ebooks are sold.

www.Harlequin.com

HARLEQUIN
Presents®

**Coming next month—escape with this
spellbinding royal duo!**

**Read *The Prince's Scandalous Wedding Vow*, Jane Porter's
deeply emotional royal romance. Innocent Josephine finds
it impossible to ignore her instant connection to mysterious
Alexander—but will his royal secret change everything?**

When Josephine rescues a drowning stranger,
she's captivated. Until it's revealed he's Prince Alexander,
heir to the throne of Aargau… Now the threat of scandal
means this shy Cinderella must become a royal bride!

**Discover *Innocent Queen by Royal Command*,
part of Kelly Hunter's sinful and sexy Claimed by a King
miniseries. His royal duty must come before anything,
but will King Augustus be able to resist temptation?**

King Augustus is shocked when his country
delivers him a courtesan. But Sera's surprising innocence
and undisguised yearning for him pushes Augustus's
self-control to the limits. Now he won't rest until
Sera becomes his queen!

Available February 2019

Want to give in to temptation with steamy tales of irresistible desire?

Check out **Harlequin® Presents®**, **Harlequin® Desire** and **Harlequin® Kimani™ Romance** books!

New books available every month!

CONNECT WITH US AT:

Facebook.com/groups/HarlequinConnection

Facebook.com/HarlequinBooks

Twitter.com/HarlequinBooks

Instagram.com/HarlequinBooks

Pinterest.com/HarlequinBooks

ReaderService.com

HARLEQUIN®

ROMANCE WHEN YOU NEED IT

PGENRE2018